I0599945

WHERE THE WATER GLOWS

The Legacy of Stan Wallace

Jamie Lee Carrie

Library of Congress cataloging-in-publication data has been applied for.

WHERE THE WATER GLOWS
The Legacy of Stan Wallace.
Copyright © 07-01-2025
Jamie Lee Carrie
All rights reserved.

ISBN: 979-8-9926590-7-8 (PB)
ISBN: 979-8-9926590-6-1 (KINDLE)
ISBN: (HB)
ISBN: (EPUB)

**I am an AMERICAN author. I speak and write in the dialogue that is prevalent in the USA, specifically, in the southern states. If you are not familiar with this dialect, I do apologize. It is not considered proper KING'S ENGLISH, but it is proper spelling and grammar for my country of origin. Some phrases may have to be googled for better understanding. I hope it does not hinder your ability to read, understand, and enjoy.

For my children—James, Jet, Joel, Stan, Landen, Tristin, Michaela & Anisette.
For my grandchildren—Alexia, Zander, Lucius, Talyiah, Mathew, Nolan & Calvin.

A special dedication to my first grandchild Matthew Lane. Rest with the angels, sweet boy. The world will never be the same without you in it.

I wrote this story with family in mind. This book is intended for everyone to enjoy. Either read on your own or share with someone you love. It should touch a place in all of us, young and old alike.

1.

The truth is that I am a writer by trade, but I've never thought myself good at it. When I was a young boy, I had always imagined pouring my heart and soul into writing great literary masterpieces. You know — to leave some great legacy behind in the form of words arranged unlike any other.

And then life happened.

Dreams were left behind and replaced with everyday survival tasks. Disillusion followed.

Before meeting *him,* I'd spent the last fifteen years working for a small-town paper proofreading and editing. Puff pieces, county fairs, and eulogies. I left the hard-hitting stuff for people who had talent. Talent that I admitted at a fairly young age I wasn't blessed with.

My career paid the bills but hadn't brought me satisfaction, at least not in the way I always imagined it would.

I married my wife, Sarah, at twenty-five and continued on the path I had marked out for the sole reason of supporting a family. We settled into a routine, and I had gotten so comfortable with it, I never considered chasing a different dream, even if I'd had one.

And I suppose that was the problem. I simply couldn't see myself doing anything else. Especially after the accident.

Of course, other things kept me happy in my free time. Hobbies such as fishing and painting, but no other job considered would give me the same stability. And so, I devoted my life to work that always fell short of being truly gratifying.

I still considered my life a good one. I was content with the mundane. It was sure and steady and appealed to my need for consistency. I never felt the call to reassess until it just seemed too late.

I said all of that so that I could say this.

Many people could have written what you are about to read. People who could have told the story differently and, I'm sure, better. But I was the one who was chosen.

Bear with me while I try my best to make a *decent* story out of what should be a *beautiful one*.

2.

I recall the day my world changed. I remember it like it was yesterday.

She came into my office on a Tuesday. I had just returned from lunch, and there she was — Red shirt, yoga pants, and a black rain poncho.

My first impression of her was muddled. She looked disheveled. Long black hair still dripping from the rain, her tennis shoes caked in mud, her glasses dotted with foggy droplets.

I could feel her energy right away.

She was like a tornado. Jerky in her mannerism, almost haphazard or desperate, as if she were running from something. My mild manner switched into fight-or-flight mode, and I pushed back the only way I knew how: energetic indifference. So, our beginning was uncomfortable, to say the least.

I stood behind my desk and watched a stranger pace through my office like she owned the place, waiting for an explanation, or at least an introduction.

She grabbed a tissue from my desk, removed her glasses to clean them, and after a few more minutes of awkward silence, she spoke.

Her first attempt came out in a rush. A rant of sorts that made absolutely no sense at all. She stopped, looked me in the eyes, inhaled deeply, and let out an exasperated sigh. Then she plopped herself down in the chair opposite mine. All the while I stood motionless, not knowing who she was or what to say.

I kept looking out at my secretary, hoping she would come in and rescue me or clue me in on who the stranger was in my office and why she'd let her in. That didn't happen.

Finally, I found my voice.

"Why don't you start by telling me your name?" As I took my seat.

She wiped her face and put her glasses back on.

She was attractive. Petite, oval face, light olive skin, and obviously of Asian descent. I studied her for a few moments before she spoke again.

"I'm Leigh. I have passed this building dozens of times and wanted to come in, but for some reason I never could, until now."

"Okay, Leigh. How can I help you?"

I was losing patience.

"I've got a story, an extraordinary story. It needs to be told."

Oh, that's what it was about. She wanted a job. A writer who wanted a break. I had dealt with that more times than I could count. Agitated, I leaned back in my chair.

"So, it's a job you're after. You know there are better ways to apply for an internship."

She looked at me. No, she looked *through* me for a minute while my words registered before replying.

"Absolutely not! I have trouble writing a grocery list. This isn't about a job."

She chuckled but seemed a bit irritated. At me, or her inability to explain, I'm not sure which. There was a long pause while she fidgeted with her poncho, trying to take it off.

I'm not sure why I sat anxiously waiting for

her to explain herself, but I did. At that point, my curiosity was piqued.

I asked,

"Can I get you something to drink? Coffee, water? I think I have some tea in the break room."

"Yes, tea would be great, thanks."

I hadn't expected her to accept, but I called the secretary to bring in a coffee and a tea. I had a feeling I was going to need it.

After a few more minutes of awkward silence, I couldn't contain myself anymore and asked again,

"So, how can I help you?"

She adjusted herself in her seat, crossed her legs, and with her fingers interlaced over her knees, she began again, that time making more sense.

"I have a friend. A friend named Stan Wallace. Have you heard of him?"

"I can't recall the name. *Should* I know of him?"

She stared at me, studying my face, as if she wasn't sure whether or not to believe me.

Donna came in with the drinks and set them down on my desk. She looked over her glasses, widened her eyes a bit and raised her eyebrows. I'm not sure what she wanted me to say. After a quick look at Leigh, she looked back at me and slightly shrugged her shoulders. With one more sideways glance, she left the office and closed the door behind her.

Leigh grabbed her cup, dunked the tea bag a few times, and discarded it on the saucer. She declined sugar and sat fidgeting with the teacup for a few minutes. Her eyes looked to the left, as if recalling, or like she had memorized the words she was about to say.

"Stan. He's a doctor living out at the bluff. He's from Santa Monica. I've written it all down for you."

She retrieved some folded pages from a small bag she had strapped around her waist and laid them on my desk. I picked them up.

"I don't understand." I said as I scanned the information on the top page.

"Look, there are dozens of people I could have approached about this, but it seems that for reasons unclear even to me, you are the one I am supposed to give this to. He specifically asked for you."

"Who? Who asked for me?"

"Stan."

"That makes no sense; I don't know him."

"I know it doesn't make sense. It's why it's taken me so long to come to you."

I leaned back with my coffee, waiting for the mystery to unfold a little more before I passed any kind of judgment.

She set her teacup down and ran her fingers across the nameplate on my desk.

"Listen, Scott... can I call you Scott?

I nodded my approval.

She looked to the ceiling for a moment, rolled her eyes, closed them, and tightened her lips. When she opened them, she stared down at the desk in front of her.

"Scott, how old would you think I am? What I mean is, how old do I look?"

I smiled. As a man, it kind of felt like a setup. I didn't answer her but sat for a moment considering her question. I looked her over

14

again with fresh eyes. I came to the conclusion she couldn't be a day over twenty-five.

For the first time, she made direct eye contact.

"Well?" she said.

I cleared my throat, still uncomfortable with going against normal societal rules.

"Not a day past twenty-five. Why?"

She abruptly stood and started fumbling with her poncho.

Surely I hadn't upset her with my answer?

After putting it back on, she pulled her long black hair into a ponytail and, while still securing it, said,

"I am 66."

I let out a short laugh. It had to be a joke, but she was dead serious, and what did her age have to do with anything?

She pointed to the pages on my desk.

"The address is on the paper. I implore you to come on Saturday; we are running out of time."

That last sentence trailed off and ended in a much softer tone, almost a whisper.

"Come early and wear good shoes. You'll have to make your way up the hillside, and the steps are in disrepair. I'll make brunch, and we can talk. If you aren't there by ten, I'll know you aren't coming and will make other plans. And Scott, come alone; he isn't comfortable with new people."

And then, like a whirlwind, she was gone.

I sat trying to digest what she'd said and what any of it had to do with me. My attention went to the pages still lying there. I looked down at them.

The first page was titled *STAN WALLACE*. It was basic information.

The second page was a bit more interesting. It was a photocopy of Leigh's birth certificate and driver's license. I looked closely. Leigh Ann Beck. Birthday: August 12th, 1956. Impossible.

The third page was a detailed map to a destination somewhere in Santa Barbara. Scribbled across the bottom was a note:

See you Saturday. DON'T BE LATE, DON'T WEAR COLOGNE, AND WEAR MUTED COLORS. Anything loud, even visually, overstimulates him.

"Overstimulates him?" *What does that even mean?*

3.

I sat pondering over what had transpired the last half hour, and, still boggled, I called Donna.

She came immediately.

"What was that all about?" she asked.

I handed her the top page and told her,

"I need you to dig up all the information you can on this guy; we'll start with him for now. I want everything– From where he was born and who his parents are to as much of his past history as you can gather; *Today*. I'll get someone else to answer the phones."

She protested,

"Scott! That isn't my job. You have loads of interns that would willingly handle this sort of thing."

"Donna, dear, please do this for me. I don't need any eager writers on this until I find out more."

She stood staring at the page in her hand.

"I'll let you have Friday off early."

She grinned.

"Deal. I'll get right on it."

As she left my office, I turned my attention back to the photocopy of Leigh's information. I still wondered if I was being played somehow and what exactly either of them wanted from me. It didn't make any sense.

By the end of the day, I was even more perplexed. Donna did what I asked, and at 6:30 I sat at my desk after most everyone had gone home and looked at the information she'd spent all afternoon collecting. To include a photo.

He stood in a group with other doctors, towering above them. Attractive enough, he was built as though he were carved out of solid rock: lean and serious.

Stan Andrew Wallace. Born in Santa Monica in 1980. His father was killed in the Gulf War in 1990, and his mother, a nurse, died of cancer in 2004. No siblings, never been married. He attended Baylor College of Medicine in Waco, Texas, where he did well, graduating at the top of his class.

All pretty normal and uninteresting stuff, until it was. *Interesting*, that is.

Apparently, Stan was a general surgeon from 2005 to 2009 in Houston, Texas — a very bad one.

Donna attached an article from Doctors Monthly magazine where a whole page was dedicated to him and his numerous mistakes and legal issues surrounding multiple deaths of patients under his care. And it didn't stop there.

Newspaper clippings told of his total and complete blackball from medicine. They had dubbed him "Dr. Death." Which culminated in a string of malpractice suits and the eventual loss of his license.

From the papers in front of me, Stan seemed to fall off the face of the planet after that.

No extra information. Other than an ad taken out in a local circulation in his name offering services as a computer/small appliance repairman dated 2011, there was nothing else, as if he had simply disappeared.

I sifted through the stack and found credit card reports. Not one transaction since 2010, and no taxes paid either. Who was this guy, and where had he gone these years?

But the question I was asking the most was, why in the world did he want to meet with me?

Was this a man who desired to tell his side of the story for some kind of redemption after all of this time?

I pulled out a bottle of Scotch I kept in my desk drawer and poured myself a drink.

While I sat thinking of all of the reasons I shouldn't go, the one reason I should was stronger. I wanted to know why he sought me out and what he wanted.

I knew before I left the office that day that I would be at that Santa Barbara location on Saturday.

4.

I arrived thirty minutes early, and it was good that I did. She wasn't kidding about the steps, and they took every bit of a half hour to navigate. With no railing and most of them all but washed out, by the time I could see the top, I was exhausted. I am not exactly into climbing, and that day it showed.

I turned to look down the incline I'd just tackled. I could see the road, but not my car. We were miles outside of the city.

I was taking a break, admiring the scenery (while trying to breathe as if I weren't dying), when I heard her.

"You made it!"

I yelled back,

"Yeah, your map was spot-on, thank God! You didn't leave a phone number."

She was near the top step, wearing a wide-brimmed hat and sunglasses, grinning from ear to ear. Her hair whipped around in the wind as she bounced on her toes. She possessed too much energy for one person. She waited while I completed the rest of the ascent.

When I finally reached the top and stepped through the gate, I was drenched with sweat. The California sun is relentless.

It took me a few minutes to catch my breath, but when I did, the view was enough to leave me breathless again. My God, it was amazing.

The land laid out before me was rectangular, flat, and narrow. So narrow that the ocean was visible on the other side. The grass was bright green and lush. There was a plantation-style home on the left with a wraparound porch and gambrel roof. It was white with black shutters and a maroon door. Meticulously kept flower beds lined the walkway and were packed with yellow and orange marigolds. A vegetable garden was enclosed with a white picket fence, and there was a constant tinkling coming from wind chimes that hung from every corner of the house.

Everywhere I looked, there was an animal.

The minute I stepped onto solid ground, I was surrounded by them.

There had to be two dozen dogs scattered about and a few puppies collected at my feet, not to mention the cats in every color and birds — so many birds chirping, in cages and without; Seagulls and chickens included.

I stood for a minute soaking it all in, not following her. Even though she was persistently pleading for me to do so.

I remained motionless, looking around, as she and a few of the dogs made their way to the porch.

There she was, hands on her hips, knee cocked, impatiently giving me time to absorb my surroundings.

Across the yard to the right was a stretch of tall yellow grass, and just past that I could see the top portion of another house. It looked more modern, art deco. A stark difference to the one I was about to enter.

I wiped my forehead with the back of my sleeve and made my way over to her, all the while she tapped her foot. That woman was so pushy without having to say a word.

I climbed the stairs and, still looking around, stumbled through the front door. I followed her a few steps before she abruptly stopped, removed her hat, and looked down at my feet.

"Shoes!" she said.

I did as I was told, leaving them by the door and quickly following her into her kitchen.

It was a long room with huge windows all of the way down one wall and half of the other, topped with white cotton curtains. Her home seemed to teeter on the edge of the bluff, overlooking the ocean. The windows allowed the most magnificent view, and I could hear the faint sound of waves crashing.

I'm not sure how long I stood there in awe before she got my attention again.

"Scott!"

I jumped at the stern use of my name.

"Oh, sorry."

She shoved a few plates, cutlery, and napkins in my hands and told me to put them on the table.

She had a way of making me feel like I was

mentally one step behind her, as if I had no common sense. Like I was inadequate because I was unsure of what was to come next. It was unnerving.

I was uncomfortable and wasn't sure if I needed to sit or be ready and available for her next order, so I lingered in between the table and the kitchen island.

She had bacon and sausages frying in one pan and eggs in the other. There was a bowl of fried potatoes and onions next to the stove as well as pancakes and French toast. Grits, wheat toast, and some type of muffin.

She finished the eggs sunny-side up and collected the meat from the pan, putting them all on a serving tray alongside huge hunks of ham. She cut up cantaloupe, strawberries, cucumber, and tomato and arranged them on a platter.

She took a batch of biscuits out of the oven and placed them on the stovetop. I watched as she sprinkled flour into the already hot skillet to make gravy; my mouth was watering.

She tipped her chin towards the finished

dishes, then in the direction of the table. My cue to take them.

I had never seen so much food. Who exactly was she feeding? I imagined my arteries clogging looking at the spread. Not that I was going to complain; the novelty of bran flakes and turkey bacon had worn off years prior. How I longed for the greasy feast in front of me. By the time I transferred everything, there wasn't a bare space left on the table.

Leigh finished the gravy and put it into a gravy boat, grabbed the biscuits, and was seated at the table before I was. I took my place across from her.

She poured orange juice into both of our glasses before reaching across the table and spearing two pancakes with her fork. She plopped them down in front of me and then got her own.

After successfully loading both of our plates, she broke the silence with a very loud and shrill scream.

"ALBERT!"

Startled, I dropped my spoon just as I was

about to dig into the grits.

Her head was turned to the entrance of the kitchen, and I followed her gaze.

I was incredibly surprised to see a child enter the kitchen.

I guessed he was no older than 5. He had on overall shorts and a blue tee-shirt, and he cradled a white fuzzy animal in his arms. He had to get closer for me to realize he was holding a bunny. It couldn't have been more than a few weeks old, and one of its tiny ears flopped over the boy's arm.

Leigh, exasperated,

"Albert, you cannot eat while holding Mozart."

She looked at him in earnest. Waiting for a reply that didn't come.

"Go put him away and wash up."

She then spoke in a language I'd never heard. Sounding short and curt. And he responded,

"Sige, Nanay."

"English." She scolded.

A bit deflated, he looked to the floor before a

quick glance in my direction.

"Okay, Mother."

As he turned to do what she'd asked of him, she tousled his thick black hair and swatted him on the behind.

She turned her attention back to the food and started to put smaller portions onto a saucer. I sat, mouth agape. At that point I was more than concerned that I was being played.

Leigh looked up briefly, put his plate aside, and started buttering a biscuit. She poured warm gravy over her open biscuits, saturated her pancakes with maple syrup, and completely covered the potatoes and eggs with chunky salsa.

I regained some sense of composure long enough to follow suit and then turned my attention back to my grits. But my mind was trying to bridge a gap between what she had told me a few days prior and what I had just witnessed. I was boggled, but not enough for it to stave my appetite.

Even after Albert joined us, we ate in silence, and in all of my years of eating food, I cannot ever remember a time when I enjoyed it more than that day. It was, without a doubt, one of the best meals I have ever had.

I finished two plates full, and I watched in astonishment as she worked on her fourth. To this day I have no idea where she was putting it!

"Do you always eat like this?" I asked.

She looked up long enough to shrug her shoulders and reach for the potatoes.

In between mouthfuls, she told Albert,

"This is Scott; he's here to see Stan. When you've finished, I want you to take him his breakfast and tell him we will be there on time. Can you do that for me?"

Albert nodded yes.

When she finished eating, she got up, put some into Tupperware, cleared the table, and served coffee. Albert left with Mozart under one arm and the container under the other.

I sipped mine while staring out the window. The ocean below was dotted with multicolored sailboats. The sun's reflection made them sparkle and it was spectacular.

I knew at some point she would speak, and I

didn't rush her.

My stomach was full, and I felt as if I needed a nap. So, I waited and tried to keep my eyes open.

5.

After a lengthy break from activity or noise, her first words startled me *again*.

"He's six."

I heard her, but it didn't register at first. She repeated it, slower and louder, as if English were my second language.

"He's six. My boy is six years old."

I leaned forward and placed my elbows on the table. More to stay awake than to try and hear her. I heard her the *first* time, but my body wasn't used to digesting that much food. It had slipped into Thanksgiving Day mode. I shook my head a little, and she responded by refilling my coffee cup.

"Okay...?" was all my brain could think of to say about her last statement.

Leigh looked amused for a minute. She knew I was past the point of curious, and it seemed that she was intentionally drawing it out for a reaction. She was studying me, measuring my doubt by my body language and answers.

She poured heavy cream into her own cup and swirled the spoon around, turning the once dark brew the color of sand. I didn't have time to consider anything else to say before she asked,

"Do you have kids?"

I folded my arms across my chest, and not wanting to elaborate further, I replied,

"I do."

Left elbow on the table, she rested her head on her hand and stared out the window. She looked down and started playing with the corner of her placemat, running her thumbnail back and forth across the corner.

She was beautiful. Not only by Western standards, but I'd say she would be considered quite lovely in any part of the world. Possessing a unique appearance that reminded me of a porcelain doll. Classic features of a bygone era. She stood about 5'4 with a delicate but healthy petite frame, and I was still clueless as to her original heritage.

Her eyes were the shade of her coffee, with a hint of green. Like muddy swamp water. The whites of them were void of any blemish or vein, as would be expected of someone over the age of thirty-five. Her lids were hooded and tilted up ever-so-slightly on the corners. The main attribute that led me to believe she was of Asian descent. Pointed chin, button nose, and long, thick, straight lashes topped with eyebrows that were perfectly arched. Olive skin; flawless. No telltale signs of age, to include crow's feet, liver spots, or even the hint of a wrinkle. Her hair was thick and shiny, waist-length, and solid black. It looked natural, not colored, and yet she had not one gray strand.

She looked up at me and smiled, displaying *Shirley Temple* dimples in her cheeks. Her teeth were straight and white, and even her hands looked to be those of a young woman.

I was looking for any evidence that she might be telling me the truth concerning her age. I was studying her hard, and she knew it.

Her return gaze was as serious as my own. It was the first time I had seen her calm. She was relaxed, and however impossible it seems to me now, it made her appear even younger.

I could have been sitting across from a nineteen-year-old girl. And maybe I was? I hadn't had any proof to the contrary yet except for a crappy photocopy of paperwork that could have been faked for all I knew. I suddenly wished I'd had Donna do some digging on her while she was at it. Leigh broke my train of thought.

"I met Stan almost twelve years ago."

She wasn't waiting for me to say anything but paused a moment as if to collect her thoughts. I could actually see her contemplating her next words. She was, for a moment, in turmoil. I didn't know *why*; I just instinctively knew she was, so I waited.

She looked out the window again and then put more words together than she had since we met.

They tumbled from her mouth, and somewhere in the midst of them she found comfort and eased into what I will refer to as a *story groove*, where she stopped over-analyzing the words themselves and simply spoke.

I hadn't yet settled into the writer alter ego of myself, and so that day I would have no recorder or notebook in hand. I am recounting this from memory.

Her tale started out simple. A quick background on her family and origins. She was Filipino, which I never would have guessed, and both parents were deceased. She had lost her only sibling, a younger brother, some thirteen years back to an illness that she didn't elaborate on.

She moved on to her education, telling me she had received her bachelor of science degree from the University of California. All pretty normal stuff, really.

She paused long enough to reach into the apron pocket she was still wearing and pull out a pouch. I watched in surprise as she rolled a cigarette, lit it, and then continued.

"When my parents were alive, their only concern was that I marry. They wanted to know I would be taken care of. My brother was still alive then, and traditionally all money or assets would pass down to him. They had that old-fashioned mind-set that I needed a man and that, for some reason, I couldn't make it on my own. Even with my academic accomplishments and the clear ability to do so. At thirty-three I finally gave in."

"I had always imagined I would marry for love, but I hadn't found it yet and loathed dating, so I relented and married a man they chose for me. Looking back, it wasn't completely about them. I'd always wanted children and didn't want to miss my "window of opportunity," so to speak.

She took a long drag of her cigarette, savoring it, letting the smoke ease out of her nostrils. She apologized as the smog headed in my direction. I shrugged it off; it didn't bother me, and in fact I secretly wanted to join her. Even though I'd quit a decade earlier, the urge never left.

"Lenny was a good man. I can say that now. He wasn't a faithful man, but good nonetheless."

"He wasn't much to look at," she grinned,

but even I could spot some anguish in it.

"But he was smart, strong, and steady. A great businessman, and in his way, he loved me."

"You must have loved him very much." I said.

My words seem to snap her out of a trance; nostalgia saturated her mood, and she looked at me blankly for a minute, allowing her eyes to refocus before replying.

"No. Sadly, I didn't."

She snubbed her cigarette out in a clamshell on the windowsill and looked to her lap. Seeming embarrassed at having said the last fact out loud.

"I learned to appreciate him for all that he was and ignore all that he wasn't."

She looked at me again, shrugged her shoulders, and said,

"We tried to have children. For years we tried. I was born with one ovary, and my eggs, even when harvested for in vitro, were deemed unusable. And even if they were, my uterus was riddled with cysts. Simply put, I was barren. I would have understood had he divorced me, but he didn't, choosing instead to have multiple affairs. Lenny died the same year I lost my brother, leaving four children behind, that I know of — all female."

At that point I was so damn confused, I didn't have a response.

Leigh sighed and stood.

"Come." She told me, and I followed her to the front porch.

She walked the length of the patio, shooing dogs, cats, and chickens away until they were all safely down in the yard, before pulling a wire mesh gate on wheels across the top step. Once latched, we both realized she had overlooked a poodle sleeping in the porch swing.

"Oh, Dixie." She said under her breath.

She rolled her eyes, scooped up "Dixie" in her arms, and placed her in her lap as she sat down. She absentmindedly stroked her and cooed.

"How are you doing today, old girl?"

She looked at me.

"What time is it?"

"11:15." I told her.

Somewhere, in between the kitchen and the porch, Leigh's demeanor changed. She had adopted a different approach.

Apparently, punctuality was of the utmost importance to *him*, and we were on a time constraint, so she gave me a whole lot of information very quickly. Information I am still, to this day, struggling to wrap my head around.

6.

After her husband Lenny passed, she met with their attorney, who spelled out for her all that was included in her inheritance. She was a wealthy woman.

Between what her parents had bequeathed and the sum of her husband's life insurance and assets, she had become that way overnight.

The lawyer shed light on many things she was unaware of, including both houses and the land around us. She had no idea they owned real estate until he told her, giving her the deeds and a map to the location. Stan was already renting the home she lived in now, and after deciding to let him stay, they'd agreed to swap.

She said the other house was too cold, angular, and pretentious for her. She felt more comfortable in the one she'd chosen. I hadn't seen the other home at that point but couldn't imagine anything more stunning than the one

I'd spent the morning in.

"It was all such a surprise to me." She explained.

"I wondered why he had kept it a secret. I assumed at the time it was so he would have a place to bring his mistresses."

She stopped petting Dixie, and her hand fell limp across the dog's little body. She looked away, focusing her attention in the direction of the other house, and said,

"And then I got sick."

That last sentence made me lean forward. Not because of what she said, but the *way* she said it. Something in the way people articulate illness — a tone, a look, I don't know; a *vibe* that completely does away with the need to ask if it's serious. You just *know*.

Once you have that feeling, usually the first instinct as a human being is to reach out and touch the one afflicted. Even if it's a simple touch on their sleeve or hand. Most feel an inner responsibility to give comfort. I'm not sure if that is a quality born in each of us or learned.

She stared back at me, not speaking for a

second, until the look on my face registered with her.

A slow grin spread across her face. A genuine smile—a smile that made it clear she understood my need to console her. She saw my empathy, and it somehow changed her. It changed *us* and the way we interacted. In those few seconds, our relationship was altered. It was a defining moment even if I cannot make enough sense of it to adequately describe it. Sincere empathy for other humans builds bridges.

"Scott, wipe that concerned look from your face; I'm alive. That was ten years ago, and I am sitting here across from you. Clearly, it didn't kill me."

She hesitated for a moment before continuing. Her shoulders relaxed, she crossed her legs and leaned back in the swing, causing the dog to jump and readjust herself. Once Dixie was settled again, she said,

"You know, I have been battling with myself these last few days on what to tell you. What I mean is…how much I should say. I've decided to tell you only what you need to know for now and allow Stan to fill in the rest."

I was still completely in the dark. Unclear as to why I was there and what it was I *needed* to know or why I needed to know it, but she had my undivided attention.

"Shortly after I lost my Lenny, I was diagnosed with pancreatic cancer. Apparently, I'd been sick a while. It was stage four, and my chances of survival were in the 10% range. I had symptoms, of course, but nothing alarming. Mainly fatigue, weight loss, and other things I simply attributed to my emotional state over recently losing the two most important people in my life.

I had what I thought to be the flu twice that year, but the second time I couldn't get out of bed for over a month. The persistent fever eventually convinced me to go to the doctor, and I learned I was terminal."

She said *"terminal"* while furrowing her brow. She inhaled deeply, exhaled, and clicked her tongue to the roof of her mouth while simultaneously shaking her head. It wasn't the kind of head shake that would normally be recognized as a silent *no*, but more like an outward display of *I still can't believe it myself.*

If I had been confused before, it was nothing compared to what I was then.

I was sitting in front of one of the healthiest-looking people I had ever met, and if she was telling the truth, and she was in fact 66, there was absolutely no way in hell she was ill. I couldn't process her words as quickly as they were spilling out at that point.

Dixie jumped down, and she eased back into the swing and put one leg underneath her, using the dangling leg to gently propel. The swing swayed back and forth, toward me — away from me. Her floral skirt flowed with the tempo, never having time to completely rest on her knee. Her eyes fixed on mine, seeming to search for the reaction I hadn't given.

She looked past me as she said,

"I decided fairly early on that I wouldn't choose treatment. I didn't want my last time on this planet to be a battle. I had lost everyone I'd ever cared for in a span of five years, and my will to continue was gone. I was fifty-six when I moved into this house, and essentially, I came here to die."

Her eyes squinted.

"Cancer is a funny thing. It's as if once it gets acknowledged, once the diagnosis is verbalized, it materializes. It comes forth in a rage, attacking with twice the veracity it had before you actually heard the words. One day I wasn't sick, and the next I was."

She abruptly planted her foot and stopped swinging.

"Within eight months I couldn't function. It took over my body at such a rapid pace I couldn't even perform daily tasks. That's when Stan stepped in."

"At first, he ran errands for me, brought me food and medicine, and helped me take care of the place. He fed the animals, tended to the yard, things like that."

"When I started to experience a lot of pain, he administered narcotics. I was bedridden most of that year, and he did all he could. I thought that would be the way it would end; I would die in a fog of morphine and pain."

Again, Leigh looked out to Stan's house. And said,

"But that wasn't the way of it."

She tucked a stray hair behind her ear as she spoke.

"One night I couldn't sleep. I'd had an especially hard day. No amount of medicine was going to help, and I lay wishing it to be over with. The pain, my life, the anguish—all of it."

Tears filled her eyes as she recalled the memory, and I couldn't take it anymore.

I moved from the old wooden rocker where I'd been and seated myself beside her on the swing.

"Sometimes, on really bad days, Stan stayed over and slept in the spare room. That night he was there, like he had been countless times before. He didn't want me to die alone any more than I wanted to."

"But on that night, he came to me. He came to my bed and lay down beside me."

"Forgive me, because my exact memory of that night is blurred from all of the painkillers, but what I do remember is that I was on my side. I was curled up in a fetal position, and he climbed in behind me and lay against my back. He cradled me in his arms like one would a small child. One arm under me, one arm over, around my waist. He had his hands on my abdomen. At first, just resting them there. But then, he pulled them inward, pulling my whole body tightly against his own."

"His hands became as hot as a stovetop. It felt like an iron poker was being thrust through my gut to my backbone."

"The pain was excruciating, and I hollered out. But he didn't stop; he held firm."

She looked at me then, directly into my eyes.

"I heard a train. As sure as we are sitting here, the sound of a steam engine was in my ears, in my brain. I was in complete agony — and then I wasn't."

Her voice trailed off.

After a moment she cleared her throat and said matter-of-factly,

"I don't know how long I slept, but it was the first time in many months I'd slept soundly, and when I woke up, I was better. I had no pain, no signs of illness. I felt normal. No; I felt much better than normal. I felt completely healthy. I felt like a sixteen-year-old kid."

I broke our eye contact and stared ahead. I wasn't sure how to respond. My mind was still trying to digest what she had told me thus far.

"Can you roll me one of those cigarettes, Leigh?"

Old habits die hard.

She immediately searched in her pocket, pulled out the tobacco, and started rolling one of two. We lit them, and as the first bit of smoke escaped my lips, I remembered how much I really liked smoking.

She gave me time to enjoy it before saying, "There's more."

"Of course there is." I said, trying not to sound sarcastic.

"Over those next few weeks things changed with my body. Each day I didn't just get better, I looked better. Every time I looked in the mirror, I looked different. Wrinkles started to dissipate, and my eyelashes, hair, and eyebrows became thick and black. Any sagging that showed in my face or jawline became tight again, and any ailments or injuries repaired themselves. My bad knee, arthritis, and even cavities I had in my teeth were gone. And at 57 I had a menstrual cycle again!"

"Those daily improvements went on for about a year, and what I am now is the final result."

"This is a lot to take in," I told her.
I had a million questions to ask but wasn't sure where to begin.

7.

I excused myself to use her bathroom. I needed a few moments to myself. To wash my face and absorb what I'd just heard.

"It's down the hall beside the kitchen, on the left."

I used her toilet, washed my hands, and splashed cold water over my face a few times, all while trying to decide what I should ask her first.

What was the most important thing to know, or what was it she could say to convince me that what she had told me was the truth? I dried my hands, replaced the towel, and came out as unsure as I was when I'd gone in.

I paused in the hallway, across from the bathroom. A photo on the wall caught my attention. It was a close-up picture, matted in black, in a beautiful ornate silver frame.

Two subjects. A very attractive-looking

gentleman, who looked to be in his mid-forties, and an older woman. I studied both of them. They were smiling, and she had her head resting on his shoulder. Her smile revealed decay between her front teeth. The longer I stared at it, the more apparent it became exactly what it was I was looking at.

Although she wore a crown of silver hair with deep-set wrinkles on her forehead and around her mouth, I knew those eyes. They were muddy swamp water, and she had dimples.

Lost in my own confusion, I didn't hear Leigh come into the house. She was suddenly standing beside me, looking fondly at the picture.

"That's me and my brother Ray a couple of years before he passed."

I fumbled with words.

"Leigh, is this *really* you? I assumed it was your mother."

She stifled a giggle.

"I was 53, I believe."

She looked at me, flashed a very amused

smile, and said,

"I know, I looked every bit of sixty years old!"

She took her apron off and hung it on the hall-tree, turned around to put her shoes on, and said,

"Sunscreen. For the life of me, I'll never understand why my generation wasn't schooled on the importance of UV protection. Can you believe we used to coat ourselves in oil and sunbathe for hours?"

She grabbed her hat on the way out the door, and while I was still getting my tennis shoes on, she said,

"Let's go!"

Realizing my questions would have to wait, I rushed to catch up.

8.

His house was further away than it looked. We followed a well-worn trail, passing a gazebo that overlooked the ocean. It was decorated with oriental lanterns that appeared to hang on for dear life against the wind. Leigh held her hat in place with one hand and her skirt down with the other.

As we neared Stan's home, I felt the shift in mood immediately. Not with her, but with the house itself.

Her earlier description of "*cold and pretentious*" was adequate enough, but I'll add the word "sterile" to complete the picture. Where hers was warm and inviting even from the outside, his was quite the opposite.

Solid taupe in color, with no shutters, no flowers, and no wind chimes. If it weren't for the tinted windowpanes, it would have blended right into the surroundings. For lack of a better word, it was boring.

She knocked three times on the right side of the oversized double door before poking her head in to announce our arrival.

We dropped our shoes outside on the landing, and I followed her in.

She tiptoed through the entryway, and I'm not entirely sure why, but I mimicked her and tiptoed close behind.

We walked down four wide steps with iron railings into a sunken living area, and it wasn't until we were completely inside of that space that the magnitude of it hit me; it was enormous. The sheer size of it bordered on vulgar.

Vaulted ceilings were accentuated with oak beams that ran vertically as well as horizontally, seeming to make a 3D grid. A three-dimensional waffle of sorts. It was one of the *coolest* things I have ever seen. Second only to the far wall, or should I say, the absence of one.

The whole back of the house was glass — as was part of the floor — allowing one to look down and beyond the cliffside through a lip a few feet into the hardwoods. The angle and position of the house gave the impression we were floating above water, as if we were on a cloud.

Though monochromatic, it was tastefully decorated and surprisingly charming. Light gray walls, black light fixtures, and everything trimmed in polished oak. Clean lines and no clutter. I looked around, and although one complete wall was built-in shelving, it was sparse. A piece of crystal, a statue of an eagle, a row of family photos all professionally framed, and what looked to be leather-bound books in individual glass enclosures. It felt grandiose until I realized that every single thing in the room was perfectly positioned.

That space gave me a feeling that was familiar. In many ways it was like the house I'd grown up in, on a much larger scale, of course. My surroundings and all of their little peculiarities were normally byproducts of someone suffering from obsessive-compulsive disorder.

My mother had OCD, and I'm not sure if that is why I recognized the signs immediately, or if anyone would — but I knew.

I suddenly understood why we'd tiptoed; we were preventing damage or scuff marks to the hardwoods.

Each picture on the shelf was at the exact same angle as the one beside it. The two chairs in the living room were identically positioned, as if a measuring tape were used to make sure they were. A mid-century modern coffee table sat in front of a beige couch of the same style. The table held another telltale sign of the disorder.

A picture book titled *"Coral Reefs from Around the World"* was perfectly placed an inch away from the squared corner; again, it looked like a ruler had been used for spacing. An oblong, unused candle sat across the top, and a square stack of coasters was on the other corner, all with the same spacing. There wasn't a speck of dust anywhere — absolutely spotless.

I felt the same way I always felt when I went home for a visit. Nervous, but also comforted. There was an odd security in an environment of such order.

In between the living room and the kitchen sat a baby grand. Appearing small compared to its surroundings. Again, not a speck of dust or even a fingerprint on the black mirror-like polished top. I had an overwhelming desire to go touch it. To run my fingers across the slick surface, to feel the cool ivory keys. I buried my hands deep into my pockets instead.

"Do you play?" Leigh asked.

She looked at me with curiosity while waiting for my answer.

Like a child who is caught doing something wrong, I blushed. I don't know why. Maybe because it felt more and more like she knew me. She easily read me and my reactions to things, and I'm quite sure she'd already guessed my answer.

I used to play, yes."

The transition lenses on her glasses had become dark in the bright room, making it hard to see her eyes.

We stood there, silently staring at each other for a moment.

It was only then that I heard Albert. Faintly,

through the wall. His voice was muffled, but what I assumed to be Stan's wasn't. It was deep and precise.

We both cocked our heads in that direction and strained to hear what they were saying.

I don't know what I expected them to be talking about. Anything other than what they were, I suppose.

They were having a full-blown argument about something mathematical. It sounded more like two college professors going at it, except one of the voices belonged to a little boy.

I raised my eyebrow and looked sideways at Leigh.

She smiled and called out to them.

"Hey, you two, it's noon! Save it for tomorrow!"

Albert appeared a minute later, struggling to open the door while still holding onto Mozart.

He walked past us, head down. Obviously upset over having to leave in the middle of something important, he disappeared into another room next to the one he was forced out of and closed the door behind him.

She took in a deep breath, filling her cheeks with air, puckering her lips to let it out before saying,

"Your turn."

I obediently followed her, a bit nervous to finally meet the mystery man.

9.

The room was much darker; my eyes had to adjust.

It smelled of furniture oil and leather, and heavy drapes covered the windows. It was a stark difference from the space we'd just left, not only in appearance but also in tone. In those few feet, the atmosphere had changed drastically. To be honest, it threw me off a bit.

The room was small and intimate, which had an odd effect. It made me hyper-aware of my own existence, causing me discomfort, if that makes sense. I stood there looking around, my hands still in my pockets. My manners all but forgotten.

He was seated in a wingback chair behind a very ornate desk. Albert had obviously occupied the matching one across from him. The child's work still lay where he'd left it.

Stan stood and collected the pages with one

hand and extended his other to introduce himself. He seemed more uncomfortable than I was; I didn't know that was possible.

My first impression of him — once the shock wore off — was that there was absolutely no way he was the man from the paperwork. No way.

Although tall and broad-shouldered, he looked to be in his seventies.

The hand I shook was wrinkled, frail, and dotted with liver spots. He wore a light blue oxford that seemed two sizes too big, and his belt, which held up his jeans, was cinched in so much so that it caused the fabric around his waist to gather.

I took Albert's place across from him.

Initially he wouldn't maintain eye contact, scanning the top of his desk a few times before having a seat. When he did look at me directly, it was with the bluest irises I have ever seen. Piercing; tired.

He held a mechanical pencil, and what I thought was intentional tapping turned out to be an inability to keep himself from shaking. Forgetting myself, I rudely stared until he dropped it and firmly covered it with his palm. He looked past me.

"Leigh, would you be so kind as to get the tea?" he asked.

I'd forgotten she was in the room.

He sat, studying me, while I looked at the wall behind him. It was a built-in bookcase that was home to hundreds of books. Neatly packed in so tightly, there was not one inch of space left. Their arrangement was not by size or subject but very obviously by color. White, black, blue, and a few darker greens; all blocked together, giving it a neat and artsy appearance. I immediately noticed the absence of red. There was no crimson, maroon, or any shade of orange either. I still find that interesting.

I squinted to see what his reading tastes were, and if I was looking to gain insight into what kind of person he was, I was sadly disappointed. They were all scientific, theological, or mathematical. The same types of books one might find in a university professor's office; no great classics.

His persona screamed anything but average.

Even if I hadn't already been schooled on certain things, I'd have known instinctively he was no ordinary man.

His desk was pristine, with no wayward paper clips or Post-its. The only things occupying the top were an old-fashioned phone (a landline), a closed textbook that I presumed was part of Albert's lesson, a Rolodex, a spiral notebook, a desk lamp, and four writing utensils. Two pens and two pencils, precisely placed side-by-side.

I shifted in my chair and waited for him to speak. After all, *he* had invited *me* there.

He leaned back, put his elbows on the arms of the chair, and interlaced his fingers, resting them below his chest.

After a lengthy and extremely awkward silence, he said,

"I know I owe you an explanation for why I brought you here, and I have thought about how to explain this to you for a very long time, but I find myself at odds about how to even begin."

Leigh lightly rapped on the door before

entering with a tray that contained a silver teapot and two cups. She placed it on the corner of the desk before going to the window and opening the drapes.

"We aren't vampires for Christ's sake," she exclaimed.

She looked us both over while going around the room to turn off the lamps. Then said,

"I'll leave you to it." And she was gone.

Stan slid his hand across the desk and pulled the tray toward him. He poured the steaming liquid into both cups; mint leaves floated to the top.

"Sugar?" he asked.

"No, thanks."

He was testing my patience, and I was about to flat out ask him why I was there and what he wanted from me when he started answering the questions I hadn't yet spoken out loud.

10.

The steam from the tea curled between us, a thin ribbon rising and vanishing as quickly as it appeared. Stan studied me with the kind of look that felt less like scrutiny and more like memorization. Like he was trying to not only see who I was but also how I was made.

"I was a different man before the water," he began. His voice had a slow precision, the cadence of someone who weighs every word like it needs to be perfect. I sat back in the chair and waited.

"I came here almost fifteen years ago on a whim. Running away from shame, from lawsuits, from a name that had become a warning label. I didn't think I had anything left to salvage."

He looked away, past the open curtains.

"I went diving alone. There's a reef, not marked on any map I've ever found. The older locals who know of it call it the *Light of Heaven*. But even though the story has been passed down for generations, none have ever seen it. There is no proof of its existence before me. I found it by accident, or maybe fate; I don't know. "

"I dove about thirty meters down before I saw it. It wasn't a creature, not exactly. It was a presence. A shimmer in the water like liquid fire, gold and silver and blue, rotating and pulsing like breath."

He paused, fingertips resting lightly on the teacup.

"I felt it call to me, beckoning. Not in words or thoughts, but I knew. It wanted something, but it offered something too."

"And what did it offer?" I asked.

He looked at me again, and this time the tiredness in his eyes gave way to something else, something mournful, as he answered,

"The ability to repair." He sipped his tea, let out a sigh, and continued.

"It asked for an acceptance; it wanted me to agree, and when I did, it pulled me in, encompassed me, and filled me with more energy than I've ever known. It felt like it stripped me of all I'd been and rebooted me mentally, spiritually, and psychologically. I was reborn that day."

"I awoke on the beach several hours later, and I coughed up the mercurial substance for days. My body was covered with it; I even cried argent tears. The power, or ability, was infused into me somehow."

"The experience was like a dream, but I had been given simple instructions and new instincts. It didn't take long to realize that I was meant to heal people, but every time I did heal, it took something from me. Not only energy, but also time, age, and strength. That part was a surprise."

"The first time, I lost a little color in my hair. The second my back started to ache like I'd done twenty years of manual labor. Now, I'm in a body that's seventy-five-*ish*. Maybe older. *Probably older.*"

I couldn't respond. My heart was pounding as a quiet horror settled in.

"Why keep doing it?" I finally managed.

He stared at me curiously, solid and serious, almost as if to say, *"why would you ask that?"* He answered a bit curtly but softened the words with a pleasant smile.

"Because those people needed me more than I needed time."

It felt like everything in the room had taken a breath and refused to let it go, including me.

He stood slowly and walked over to a cabinet behind his desk. He pulled out a folded piece of paper, yellowed and soft from handling, and offered it to me.

It was a photo of a toddler held by a young, stocky woman with high cheekbones and eyes like mine. Her beauty was hard to overlook. Her other hand rested on the shoulder of the second boy, possibly in his early teens.

"That's you," Stan said, pointing to the child in the woman's arms.

The room shifted under my feet.

"Our mother's name was Irene. You were given up during a very bad time, when we had nothing. My father died, yours left, and she couldn't care for us both. I was old enough to fend for myself, but you were taken by the state, and I never saw you again. Not until Leigh showed me your byline in the paper."

The room blurred at the edges.

Not because I was unaware that I was adopted or that I didn't know my biological mother's name; neither was news to me. But that was the first time I'd seen a picture of her, and until that moment, I had no idea I had a sibling.

"I didn't contact you sooner because I wanted to be sure, but I knew, and I also knew what needed to happen next."

"And what's that?" I asked, still staring at Irene.

He looked down at his hands, now trembling even at rest.

"It has to pass on. The ability. The cost. The purpose. It was never meant to stay with one man forever, and it calls for blood—a vessel. I can teach you if you're willing to carry the weight. But for me, with my past, it didn't feel like a calling; it felt more like the possibility of redemption. I can say with certainty, it would be different for you. And, through you, I know that it must live on."

I pried my eyes from the photo and looked at him. The space between us suddenly felt like it had shrunk.

"You came here to write a story," he said. "But you were always part of it."

And in that moment, I felt it: a quiet shift. A buzz in the air that hadn't been there before. As if something had lifted, and because it was all out in the open, there was relief for him and fear and confusion for me.

11.

Sleep did not find me that night. Not fully. I lay in the unfamiliar bed Leigh had prepared in her guest room, eyes to the ceiling, my mind running laps in the dark.

He said we shared blood. He said I was chosen. He said it must pass on and I believed him. Not because I wanted to, but because honesty has a particular weight to it, and everything about that room — his hands, his words, that weathered photograph — was saturated with truth.

In the still hours of the early morning, I rose and found myself staring out the bedroom window. The moon hung low and full, and silver light bled into the garden below. Somewhere down the slope, past the marigolds and tall grass, Stan slept — or tried to. Maybe he lay as I did, wide-eyed, waiting for dawn.

By the time the sun slipped over the horizon,

I'd made my way to the porch. Leigh was already there, seated cross-legged on the swing with a mug cupped in her hands. She looked at me without surprise.

"You didn't sleep," she said simply.

"Not a wink."

She patted the space beside her, then poured a second mug from a thermos and handed it to me.

"He told me everything," I said.

She nodded slowly. "He needed to."

"And you believe all of it?"

Leigh turned to me, her eyes uncommonly soft and still. She was a completely different person than she had been days before. Just like Stan, it was as if she'd waited years for the relief that would come from letting the secret go, and it had finally come.

Anticipation over, she no longer bore the weight of it as she replied.

"I didn't believe it at first. Until the pain was gone and the mirror lied in my favor. Until Albert."

It was so quiet, the kind of silence only early

mornings know how to be. The kind that's contemplative.

"He's dying, isn't he?" I asked.

"Yes," she said. "Faster now."

"And I'm supposed to replace him."

Leigh looked toward the ocean.

"You don't have to. You have a choice."

"But you don't really think I will walk away from this, do you?"

She met my gaze and teased.

"No, Scott. I think you're already halfway out the door."

Her remark deserved a laugh I couldn't muster. I finished my coffee, heart tight, nerves frayed. I didn't know how to prepare for what came next, or how to reconcile that the story, once just another strange assignment, had turned into my inheritance.

By mid-morning, Stan summoned me again. Leigh walked me to the door of his home but didn't go inside. She placed a hand on my arm.

"He'll be weaker today, but you need to be honest about things. He'll respect that."

I agreed.

The door squeaked on its hinges as I opened it, and Leigh was correct. He was seated at the same desk, though his frame had shrunk somehow. His sweater hung looser on his shoulders and he looked exhausted.

"Good morning," I said.

He replied by telling me to sit.

"You have questions," he said.

"Too many."

"Then ask."

I leaned forward.

"Why me? And don't say it's because we're brothers. I need the truth, the complete truth."

He studied me for a long time before answering.

"Because you're built for it. I watched from afar. The way you handled the loss of your family. Quiet strength, Scott. You never sought the light, but you carried it, and that matters."

He knew. Stan had to know about the accident. I pushed it from my mind as soon as the memory tried to rush in. Then asked,

"What will it feel like?"

He clasped his hands together and looked

down at them.

"From experience I can only describe it to be like lightning or drowning. Like fire, until it settles in, or until you find balance."

He opened a drawer and withdrew a small, silver vial.

"The transfer begins with this. It will hurt. Not your body—but your memories. You'll see and feel everything I've seen and felt. It's part of the collection from my last dive. I was never able to go back again, and this is all that I have left. I will transfer the rest to you through my hands."

I stared at the vial. My heart beat like a drum.

"If I say no?"

"I die, and the gift fades. Perhaps forever."

He pushed it across the desk. I couldn't take my eyes off of it, but I didn't touch it.

"Not today," I said. "But soon. I need to understand it first. I need more time."

He put the vial away.

"I was hoping you'd say that. Come back tomorrow; we'll try then."

As I stood, I felt the weight of something odd settle over me — something like responsibility or acceptance.

I had come to write a story, but instead, I would live one.

I understood what I hadn't before. Some stories don't end; they are passed down. Inherited like birthrights, estates, or blood, and we get to choose what we do with them.

12.

The rain came soft that afternoon, just enough to pattern the windows in Stan's study. Outside, the world was dulled to a muted gray, and the hush of the drizzle gave the room an uncomfortable quality that made me fidget.

Stan sat back in the leather chair, blanket pulled up to his waist. I lingered by the window for a while before he spoke.

"Scott," he said without opening his eyes, "you've been pacing that same stretch of floor for ten minutes."

I turned. "I can't stop thinking."

He smiled. "Then sit, and ask what you came to ask."

"Was it God?" I asked. "The power and the healing. *Is it from God?*"

Stan opened his eyes. There was a long pause when he said nothing. He looked at me as if I'd asked something he hadn't considered, but

I knew better.

"I don't know," he said finally. "I used to think so. In the beginning, it felt divine…like grace in physical form. But then I started questioning."

"Because of the cost?"

"Because of the silence," he replied. "God, as we're taught, speaks. He comforts and reassures. This power never did; it simply *was*. It never told me why or how, and it didn't come with commandments. Just a knowing and an undeniable pull."

"I laid hands on a child with terminal lymphoma and watched her body restore itself overnight. Her parents fell to their knees, crying, *'Hallelujah,'* but afterward, I was in bed unable to move for days, and there was no voice from above, only pain."

"But you kept doing it," I said.

He nodded.

"Yes, I kept doing it, because even while suffering, it felt right. Like a perfect purpose or calling. But was it *God* or something older? Something buried under the names we give it?"

I sat down close to him.

"Do you believe in God?"

"I believe something made us, and I believe it watches. But whether it interferes, I'm no longer sure. This force I carry, it feels ancient. It doesn't ask for faith, and it doesn't demand worship; it simply moves through me, through sacrifice and connection."

I didn't let that sit between us nearly long enough before asking,

"Then how do you know who to help?"

He exhaled.

"I don't, not exactly. I feel pain that's not mine; it's theirs. It comes like static at first, a low bout of suffering that rises over days, and when it's strongest, they come. Sometimes I know their name before they arrive, and I add them to the ledger, but that's rare."

"And when you do get a name?"

"Those are usually people I'm tied to," he said. "Always blood or bond, family, or possibly soulmates. The ones whose suffering echoes through the deepest part of me. I don't even choose — *it* chooses me, or maybe we choose each other."

He paused, then added,

"I've come to believe that pain carves a path, and that path, no matter how long it takes, is how we find each other."

We sat for a moment.

With revelation, the room echoed a sound similar to that of a dog whistle, a high-pitched tone, and a sharp ringing in my ears.

"So, it's not some divine register?" I asked as I stuck my finger in my ear and moved it around, trying to scratch the tickle. "No angel whispering names into your ear?"

Stan chuckled.

"I wish. It's more like gravity. Pain has weight, and it pulls. If you're sensitive enough, if you're open the right way, you feel it."

"And when that happens?"

"You answer, or you don't. But if you don't, it doesn't go away. The pain festers and eats at you until you either heal or go mad."

He leaned forward slightly, grimacing as his joints popped, and said,

"You'll know soon enough."

He cleared his throat, unintentionally stressing the importance of his next words.

"The first one you heal begins in the heart, where you're the weakest. Where you're softest. It will happen naturally, without effort or a need for direction, but it will hurt the worst. It will be an illness you have had an intimate encounter with, and that's how it knows you're ready. When you welcome the angst and the pain you've already had experience with. When you choose to help, knowing how bad it is going to hurt, you *choose* love."

"And after that?"

"It doesn't get easier," he said. "But it gets clearer."

I looked down at my hands. My palms itched suddenly, as if my body were already anticipating what they might do one day.

Stan's voice softened.

"Scott, if you're afraid, that's good; it means you're not taking it lightly."

"I don't even know what 'it' is yet."

He smiled again. "Then you're exactly where I was."

Rain tapped against the window, echoing around the little room. Stan leaned back, and I could see the extra exertion of the day in his body language.

I rose. "Get some rest."

But as I reached the door, he added something that stopped me.

"If it is God, then he hides himself in suffering, and maybe that's the point. Maybe finding Him means walking straight through the pain."

My hand was on the doorknob, but his last words captured my attention and I turned around. His eyes were closed again, but I knew he wasn't asleep yet.

I stepped out of the room; the weight of all that he'd said echoed in my head as I leaned against the living room wall.

I didn't know if the gift came from God or something else entirely, but I knew that whatever it was, it was calling. And, at that point, I also knew I was open to it.

13.

The big house creaked louder.

I had come to recognize its nighttime sighs as more than groans of settling wood. It was almost as if the place breathed with Stan. Every creak a cough and every groan a wince.

Stan hadn't left his room in three days.

I stood in the doorway, watching the man who once seemed carved from mountain rock curled up beneath a faded quilt. A damp cloth sat in a bowl on the nightstand, and beside it, a heavy book with yellowed pages lay open. Stan had once called it the *ledger*, though I'd never seen him write in it, only silently read.

"Still breathing." I said under my breath.

Stan stirred and opened his eyes.

"And you're still here?" he asked.

"I am."

He gave me a weak grin.

"You should've run when you had the

chance."

I brought a chair closer, setting it beside the bed.

"I tried a few times, but something keeps yanking me back."

"Good," Stan whispered, "it means it's working."

"What's working?"

Stan closed his eyes, and for a minute I thought I'd lost him, but he spoke again.

"I was so confused at first; I didn't know what it was in the beginning. I thought I was losing my mind. I couldn't sleep and I couldn't ignore pain I didn't own."

"A girl in Phoenix had leukemia, and I felt it weeks before I met her. I healed her, but at the time I still didn't understand how; I just knew what to do. I put my hands on her and the last thing I remember is how damn hot my palms felt, as if I'd dipped them into boiling water — almost intolerable. I woke up in the hospital three days later. I was amazed that I didn't have blistered fingers, but I couldn't walk for a week. I don't know why it was so rough on me at first."

He let out a brittle laugh that ended with a cough.

"They told me I was dehydrated and vitamin deficient. Doctors need their boxes."

"You gave her your strength," I said.

"More than that, I gave her my years."

My hands unwillingly clenched into fists in my lap. I looked at Stan's face, the gray wisps in his beard, and the translucence of his skin. He looked like death was breaching the contours of his soul.

"You said once you were seventy-ish." (I already knew better, but I had to circle back.)

"I was born in 1980; you do the math."

"That would make you… what, forty-six?"

He didn't reply.

I stood abruptly, nearly knocking the chair over, and stepped away from the bed.

"That's not possible."

"No." Stan agreed. "It shouldn't be."

Silence fell between us again, not because I didn't have more to say, but because I felt like I would let him down by speaking the words aloud. After gaining the courage, I told him the truth.

"I'm not ready for this."

He answered, "I know."

"Then why now, and why me?"

Stan's eyes opened again, sharp this time.

"Because I felt you long before I found you again. You're tied to this, Scott—to *me*, to all of it."

I turned away. I was staring at an old rustic farmhouse painting as I shamefully admitted,

"I don't want to be some mystical mule for other people's pain."

"That's not what this is," he said, strength rising momentarily in his voice. "it's not about carrying their pain. It's about seeing it and feeling it and knowing what to give without killing yourself."

I turned around, scanning his frail figure.

"You don't look like someone who figured that part out."

"I didn't have help." Stan wheezed. "You will."

He motioned toward the ledger on the

nightstand.

"Take it."

A bit hesitant, I reached for the book. It was heavier than it looked, bound in cracked leather, the cover unmarked. I opened it to the first page. A name, a date, and a single word: *Repaired.*

Inside were many names, ages, dates, and conditions. Each line told the story of a human being who had been restored from terminal illness, broken spines, or end-stage organ failure. Some were dated years back; others just weeks. Page after page followed with dozens, maybe hundreds, of names, and each ended with the same word: *Repaired.*

Toward the back, the entries changed, and the handwriting became sloppy. The final few were incomplete. One read: *Scott H.*

"Is this me? Did you put *me* in the ledger?"

"I felt you," Stan whispered. "Like a missing part of myself. I couldn't place it until you walked through my door. You aren't sick; it was a different pull."

Momentarily relieved, I closed the book and reclaimed my chair.

"Why didn't you tell me sooner?" I asked.

"Would you have listened?"

I didn't have an answer.

He coughed again, this time deeper.

"How long do you think you have?" I asked.

"Not long enough to waste words, but maybe enough to finish what we started."

I nodded and slowly reached for Stan's hand. The moment our palms touched, I felt it — a strange, low-frequency vibration — not only through my fingers but also in my stomach, in my chest, and in my bones. Neither pain nor power — just an exchange.

I quickly withdrew my hand. Every hair on my body stood up, and my ears were ringing.

"What in the world do I do with *this*?" I asked, voice hoarse.

"You learn," Stan whispered, "you listen, and you stay human."

I closed my eyes. Somewhere, far away, a siren wailed. Closer, the wind rustled against the windowpanes. But inside, the air between us changed, a subtle rearrangement of energy, like a tide shifting. I sat absorbing it, trying to juggle the overwhelming feeling that, for a few minutes, I was filled with electricity.

Stan had fallen asleep, his breathing faint but steady.

Open again, the ledger rested in my lap and the words on the pages seemed to flicker in the low lamplight. *Repaired. Repaired. Repaired.*

But none of it felt final.

Something unfinished lingered between those pages, between him and me, and I felt something coming.

I didn't know *what,* but I would soon enough.

14.

The next day came dressed in a heavier quiet.
Not the kind born from peace, but from a
knowing. Something had changed, something
was being asked of me, and though I wasn't
ready to say yes, I was far past the point of
saying no.

I spent the morning pacing Leigh's porch,
watching the sky shift over the horizon. Clouds
moved in from the west, thick and layered.
There was a breeze that hadn't been there the
day before, and it smelled of *wet soil* and *longing*.
Does it make sense for those two things to reside
together in one sentence? It does for me.
Something was tugging at my soul, and I was
pulling away from it, even though I knew it was
a losing battle.

Leigh didn't speak much, but she was
nearby, singing while pruning the marigolds.
Albert rode his bicycle around the front yard,

with Mozart tucked into the basket as though the little rabbit were used to morning rides.

I watched them, the odd beauty of their lives. Watching them go about their daily activities brought me comfort. I felt like an outsider pressed against glass.

By 10:00, Leigh handed me a satchel. Inside was a small notebook, a pen, a bottle of water, and a wrapped sandwich.

"You might want to write things down," she said.

I nodded, though I didn't quite understand what she meant yet.

"And eat something afterwards. You'll need it."

I gave her a long look, and she gave nothing away. The tornado inside of her, from the first time we met, was nowhere to be found. Although her hands were always busy, the weight was lifted, and she'd become calmer.

Stan's door was already open when I got there. That time, I didn't knock; I just stepped inside and removed my shoes at the threshold.

The house was dimmer than before, the

curtains drawn tighter, as if shielding its occupant from too much of the world. The vampire statement Leigh made before ran through my mind.

I passed his open bedroom door first and looked in. Impeccably clean and tidy, but empty.

He was in his study sitting at his desk, the vial between his hands, his fingers wrapped around it tightly. His face looked paler; his eyelids and the skin along his jaw sagged more noticeably than the day before — the man was aging by the hour.

"Come in," he said without looking up.

I crossed the room and sat.

"Are you ready?" he asked.

"I'm here."

He took that as assent.

"This will not be like anything that you've known. It will feel like dying. There's really no other way to describe it; I do apologize for that. Just know that you will be fine."

He unscrewed the vial and tipped it into a small cup. The liquid inside shimmered. Unlike water, it was more like oil or mercury when heated. He handed it to me.

"Drink it quickly."

My fingers closed around the cup, and I looked at him one last time.

"What if I come out different?"

"You will," he said, "but not in the way you fear."

I drank.

It was like swallowing sunlight. It hit the back of my throat and ignited. Not in heat, but in presence. A wave of sound crashed through my brain and behind my eyes. My stomach clenched and my chest felt tight. I gasped and gripped the sides of the chair as my vision shattered into streaks.

Then came the falling.

I was no longer in the chair; I was nowhere. Then I was in water, black and warm, sinking and then light again, then darkness, and then my head flooded with memories that weren't mine.

I saw a little boy crouched behind a curtain, watching our mother cry into a pillow. I saw hands shaking over a first incision and I saw

Leigh's face the night he found her fevered, her body limp. I saw pain, regret, and triumph, and then hundreds of faces flashed before me, some smiling and others sobbing. I felt bones knit under my fingertips, tumors dissolve, and blood cleaned. I felt their joy, their fear, and then I felt his loss.

Every healing took something from him. A minute, an hour, a piece of cartilage, or pigment from his hair and clarity from his mind. Time was pulled from him, like water from a dishrag, and then faster and faster, like an open drain in a bathtub.

When I finally returned to myself, I was on the floor drenched in sweat. My breath came in uneven gasps, my throat was sore, and my legs were weak.

Stan stood above me, arms trembling as he helped me sit up.

"It's done," he said.

I couldn't speak yet; I could barely move, but I felt it: a heat in my palms and an ache in my bones.

He handed me a towel and let me rest

against the wall.

"You'll know when it's time to use it, and how."

"How long do I have before it starts?" I asked.

"It already has."

Outside, thunder rolled far in the distance, and rain pounded on the roof.

I was no longer just a man. I was something more or something less, and I felt both — simultaneously.

The light had passed into me, and I had no idea what to do with it.

I didn't go back to Leigh's house right away. My legs could barely carry me, and my mind felt like it had been scraped raw. So I stayed in Stan's empty living room, curled on the couch, exhausted. I was so weak.

The house was silent, but it felt like something inside its walls had shifted to accommodate me, or perhaps it was the new consciousness I'd swallowed.

Stan slept, and he needed to. I could hear him breathing from his room, short and shallow.

I didn't have the strength to check on him, but I knew he was alive—barely. He had given me what remained of his light, or what he could still pass of it through his hands.

I stayed until sunset.

Leigh found me, hours later, wrapped in a blanket I didn't remember pulling over myself. She said nothing but handed me a thermos of warm broth and sat down close. I drank slowly, grateful for her company.

"You'll feel strange for a while," she said after some time. "The body doesn't quite know what to do with it."

I nodded. I felt like my skin didn't fit, like it was borrowed. I was uneasy.

"How long until it settles?" I asked.

"According to Stan, it never really does," she answered. "You learn to adjust."

15.

That night, I didn't dream. Not in the way I used to. What came instead were impressions, flashes both seen and heard, and the sensation of someone else's sorrow permeated me. I felt pulled toward something, though I couldn't name it. I was a tuning fork humming against an invisible guitar.

The next morning, Leigh led me out to the garden, where there was someone waiting.

A woman, about forty, with a scarf wrapped around her head. Fragile and pale, she sat on a bench holding one of the cats; her eyes locked onto me the minute I stepped into view. She wore a look of desperate hope.

Leigh leaned in close.

"She's dying," she whispered, "from ovarian cancer. She has maybe a week."

I looked at the woman again and at the way she was trying to soothe the animal in her lap with no energy to do so.

"Why is she here?" I asked.

"Because Stan said you were ready."

I wanted to run away. I definitely wasn't ready. My body still ached, and my heart still quivered from what I'd seen and what I'd felt. I didn't even know how to begin.

"I can't," I said, "not yet."

Leigh pleaded,

"Then sit with her, listen to her, and let her feel seen. That's part of the work too."

Nervous and unsure, I walked over and introduced myself.

She told me her name was Marina. She had two daughters, both in college, and she had been a music teacher. She loved pink roses and thunderstorms and hated silence.

We talked for over an hour.

She cried, but only once. When she made jokes or spoke of funny things, I laughed, but it felt wrong in my mouth, like a nervous tic.

What I've discovered since is that people who are terminal worry about making others uncomfortable. They feel an odd sense of guilt for something that is completely out of their control, and so they make jokes, or tell funny stories, or develop a sarcastic edge for banter.

I let her know that she was safe with me, and she didn't have to talk if she didn't want to. She looked relieved and went quiet.

When she grew tired, I helped her lie down on a blanket spread over the grass. Her breathing was shallow as she reached out her hand.

"Do you think it'll hurt?" she asked.

I didn't know what she meant. Dying? Or being healed?

"No," I said. "Not the part that matters."

I didn't plan what happened next; my hands moved on their own. I placed them over her lower abdomen, where she told me the tumors were. I was flooded with warmth, not from within but from something passing through me—as if I were no more than a window the sun had chosen to enter.

I heard nothing and I saw no visions. I only felt, and when I opened my eyes, Marina was asleep.

Her breathing was deep and steady, and color had returned to her cheeks, but I felt dizzy. A part of me — the smallest part — felt dimmer, and Stan was right; it hurt like hell. It felt like a thousand heartbreaks.

When she'd gone, Leigh helped me back into the house, and I slept for a long time, and when I woke, it was dark and I felt a bit lost. I hadn't seen Stan that day.

He was isolating, waiting for his end, the one and only thing I was sure of.

It was as if he was waiting long enough to see the light move on. After that day, I was the repairman, and everything inside me knew it had only just begun.

***

The next morning, Albert waited on the porch with a book too big for his hands. He handed it to me without a word and walked toward the gazebo, and I followed. Leigh watched from the steps, arms folded, eyes shining with a mix of trust and amusement.

"Are you sure?" I asked.

"He wants you to teach him, and Scott, whether you know it or not, you've already started."

So, I did, or at least I tried.

I taught him geography, reading, and science. But mostly, I taught him things I'd never taught my own children, the things I wish I'd known before finding out the hard way.

I told him about observation, how to read body language, how to ask questions, and how to wait and listen. He started calling me "Uncle Scott," and I didn't correct him.

16.

Grief has a way of hollowing you out in silence. It doesn't shout or weep, at least not at first. It lingers behind your heart and settles in the pelvis, lower back, neck, and spine, making it hard to stand upright without being reminded that something is missing or lost.

That's what it was like waking up without Stan present but having all of his memory and pain inside of me. It was weird.

Leigh didn't say it aloud, but she felt it.

Mozart sat motionless in his corner, ears twitching toward sounds no one else heard, and Albert rode slower that morning, his bicycle cutting softer lines through the damp grass. Even the animals that normally ran to and fro were quiet, calm, and still. We were all in limbo.

I sat on the edge of the guest bed, hands clasped together, the smell of cedar thick in my nose. My body still tingled with remnants of the light, but Stan's absence left it colder, as if we drew strength and warmth from one another.

Leigh knocked softly before entering.

"I made tea."

I nodded and followed her into the kitchen. She poured two cups, and said,

"He wrote something for you."

She handed me a folded sheet of paper. The handwriting was unmistakably his, sharp, slanted, and messy.

I took it from her and read,

Scott,

This isn't a gift. It's a responsibility. If you carry it like a blessing, it will ruin you. If you carry it like a burden, it will own you. Let it be a part of you, but not all of you.

You're not meant to save everyone; you're meant to show them that healing is possible.

That's enough.

Stan.

My hands fumbled as I folded the letter and slid it into my back pocket.

"What do I do now?" I asked Leigh.

She studied me over her cup. "That depends, do you want to continue?"

"I don't know."

"Then you need to figure it out, because people will come whether you're ready or not.

She stood, and set her cup in the sink, saying,

"I'm going to check on him."

I was left alone with the sound of wind chimes and a ticking clock.

***

I didn't go back to town. I called into work and told them I was taking my long overdue personal, accumulated sick, and vacation days off, and after that, time seemed to stand still.

Leigh kept the outside world at bay, giving me room to process. I wandered the sand trails beside the house and found a place to climb down to where the water met the rocks.

I stood on the edge, staring into the black

current, next to the beach, with the memory of that bright and impossible light etched in my soul.

I wondered how close I was to the spot where it all began; I wondered if it would call to me. If it ever called to Stan, if it called to anyone at all, or if we were just broken people desperate for something to fill the cracks.

A week passed, and then two. I went to Stan in the evenings to read to him or listen to his advice when he felt up to it, but it was different. It was as if he was already gone. I knew how much he longed to be and it showed; he was just biding time.

Then, I was sweeping the porch one day when I saw a woman step through the front gate. She wore a long gray coat despite the sun, and her eyes darted as if she were uncomfortable in her own presence. Like she'd expected to be turned away.

I immediately noticed that, and it bothered me. Love should be shared, not feared, in any circumstance.

"Are you him?" she asked.

"Depends on who you're looking for."

"The one who…"

She didn't have to continue, and I didn't answer verbally; I just stepped aside and opened the door.

Her name was Evelyn and she had lupus. Years of pain engraved into her joints. She had tried everything — doctors, specialists, shamans in South America — and nothing worked. She was tired of fighting and hoping.

I listened to her speak, as I had with Marina. I made her tea, offered her a blanket, and let her feel the sun through the window. It was all I knew how to do.

When I finally placed my hands on her, I didn't think. I let the light come on its own, not forced or conjured. I allowed it to move through me like empathy through the tubes of a dialysis machine. Gently, naturally, lovingly. She sighed and closed her eyes, and when it was over and she left, her shoulders were straighter, and her hands were steadier.

That night, I wept. Not for her, not even for Stan. I wept because something inside me had shifted, and I wasn't afraid anymore. I would still ache, and I would still weaken, but I understood.

This wasn't about curing illness; it was about presence. It was about showing up fully, unguarded. It was about standing in the doorway between pain and peace and holding it open wide enough for someone else to walk through.

Leigh left a new journal beside my bed the next morning.

The first page read:

Repairman, take notes.

17.

There was a rhythm forming, though I hadn't meant to find it. I'd put in my resignation through email from Albert's computer, which I am sure left Donna quite confused. I didn't have the energy to do anything except pursue my newfound purpose.

People came. Not many, but enough to keep the house from being too quiet. They never came in groups but always arrived one at a time, as if fate took appointments.

They came with their pain, their questions, and their need to be seen — and I did what I could.

Sometimes the healing came through my hands, and sometimes it came by listening. I was learning that not all wounds were made for the light. Some needed time and touch, whereas others needed truth.

One morning, Leigh asked me to go with her

into town; supplies were low, and I needed clothes. I hadn't been back since everything changed.

The market, the stores, the square, and the grocers all looked the same, but I felt different.

Faces I once passed without a second thought now lingered in my awareness. Pain and loss were everywhere, but so were love, joy, and longing. It all pulsed in the spaces between conversations, in the slouch of a shoulder, the tremor in a hand, or tension in their neck and jaw. And people just seemed drawn to me and wanted to talk.

I helped an older gentleman carry bags to his car. His name was Walter, and his wife had died two weeks earlier. He didn't cry but spoke of her like she had only stepped away for a minute.

"She loves these pears," he said, holding one up to the sun.

I didn't heal him; I just stood with him, and perhaps that was enough. It sure felt that way.

18.

Later that afternoon, while Albert and I practiced cursive at the picnic table, I heard the gate squeak on its hinges. It was Donna.

It had been several weeks, and without questioning all that was going on around us, she had become a regular visitor.

Her hair was tied up. She wore her usual short coat and carried a paper sack of groceries, but she moved slower, as if her joints were stiff or she was overexerted.

She smiled, but it didn't reach her eyes.

"You look like a damn farmer," she said.

I laughed and hugged her.

As she sat with Leigh drinking tea, I watched her hands shake. She rubbed her temples more than once, and her complexion was paler than I remembered.

The things I noticed unintentionally when it came to people were overwhelming.

She didn't mention being ill, and I didn't ask, but right then — I knew.

That knowing settled into my ribs like the injury it was. I would address her truth when she was ready.

But I need to talk about it now.

***

Yes, Donna *was* my secretary. But she is so much more.

She has been a thread woven tightly through every season of my life, so seamlessly that I didn't notice where she started and I ended.

She was ten years my senior, and when I was a child, she'd babysit me from time to time.

My adopted parents were Susan and Bernard Harper. They were respectable, structured people. They were good, if not a bit cool in their affection.

They were social climbers, polished and poised, and they took me in later in their lives when I was already developed in many ways.

There were expectations: that I would be

disciplined, high-achieving, well-mannered, and never — *God forbid* — ordinary.

When I married young, they recoiled, because they didn't approve of Sarah. They didn't like that I settled too soon and didn't understand why I didn't choose someone more polished, more...*like them*.

My wedding became the fault line. The rift that opened was never closed, and so, Donna became my family.

Not because I asked her to, and not because she had to, but because she wanted to.

She simply loved us. Me, Sarah, and later the kids. She showed up with meals, with advice, and with wisdom we needed to hear. She came to soccer games and dance recitals, and she sat at my kitchen table drinking coffee and talking about nothing for hours. She filled the space my parents left behind. More than that, she filled it without trying to.

Donna had a family of her own. She'd married her high school sweetheart, William, and they had two children: Charlie and Chloe. I knew them, of course. They were at every important occasion in my life, and I in theirs, but I didn't know everything.

When I started working for the paper, Donna had already been the long-time assistant to the Chief editor that I would replace.

Truth be told, I got the job because of her. She vouched for me, trained me, and kept me from making a fool of myself on more occasions than I care to count. Sharp as a tack, quick with a joke and fiercely protective, Donna is the sister I never had. Secretly, I've often imagined that we *were* related…as if willing it could make it so.

But what I didn't know then was what Donna was carrying behind her steady voice and easy smile.

Donna was sick. Donna had been sick *for years*. She'd known about her diagnosis long before the first miracle touched our lives.

She never confided it to me, not because she didn't trust me or doesn't trust me, but because she loves me too much to make me worry. That is her way; she never burdens the people she loves.

She'd heard of Stan. She *had* heard whispers

in recent years of what he could do, and still, she kept her secret.

Of course she wanted to be healed, but she didn't *need* to be. That choice—her decision to wait, to quietly endure—was not born in a single moment of nobility. It was made over long, quiet years of soul-searching.

She chose us. Our friendship. My family and her family. She chose to be near without asking for more, and that is the kind of woman she is.

She has been my stand-in mother, my steady adviser, my greatest cheerleader, and the quiet hand that held mine through the darkest of times. It was her unwavering belief in me, long before any miracle ever occurred, that made room in my spirit to even imagine a different kind of life. Donna saw me at my lowest and never left.

She believes in the gift, not because it makes sense, but because it's *me*, and she's always believed in me.

It's hard to explain the kind of bond we shared for so much of my life, but if you had ever seen us together, you wouldn't need an explanation.

It's clear. Donna isn't *like* family; she *is* family by every measure that matters. We even resemble one another.

And now I must leave this chapter here.

You'll understand why this was so important later on. You'll come to see what her quiet courage has meant, but if there is one thing I hope you carry with you, it is this: Donna was never *just* a secretary, to me or anyone else who has known her.

She is the proverbial lighthouse in the storm. She's a quiet keeper of truths and a woman who gives more than she ever asks in return.

She is my friend, and she is extraordinary.

19.

That night, when I went to return Albert's drawings to his desk, I found an old photo of Leigh and Stan stuck between the pages of one of his books. Stan was younger but unmistakably them, and she was pregnant.

I brought the picture out to ask Leigh about it, and she answered immediately.

"Albert is ours," she said. "Mine and Stan's. He's your nephew."

I could not and did not hide my surprise.

"It only happened once; we were both in a lonely space." She said, blushing.

She looked a bit embarrassed as she elaborated. Not about her son, but more about keeping it from me.

"Albert doesn't know. He thinks Stan is just a friend, a neighbor that's more like a grandfather, but our boy has the gift, Scott. He's had it since he was three."

I sat down hard.

Leigh elaborated.

"It started with a dog. On a stormy night, we were driving back from town and a stray ran out in the road and Stan hit it."

"Albert screamed until we stopped. He jumped out of the car too fast for us to react. He cradled that broken animal in his arms, and when Stan reached down to move the body, it was breathing."

She wiped her eyes.

"We didn't think it was possible, but after that, it kept happening... dead birds or dying rabbits, and a ferret once; he'd pick them up, and they'd live."

"And all these animals?" I asked, sweeping my arm wide and looking around.

"They started coming to us. Sick, broken things. He can't walk past anything injured, sick, or dying, and he doesn't know why... he just saves them."

"But they don't all heal properly," she added, voice low, in a serious tone.

"The first one, Pepper, the dog we hit, he

WHERE THE WATER GLOWS

lived, but something was off. He became violent and wild, like the light didn't belong in him. He tried to attack the cats and he bit through the fence to get to the rabbits or chickens."

"Then one night, he crashed through Stan's window near his front door. Glass was everywhere, and he was bleeding, but it didn't stop him. He couldn't get close enough to the source. Like he desperately needed something he didn't understand. The last I saw of Pepper, he'd managed to hurl himself out of that glass wall in the living room to the ocean down below."

"What happened?"

"Stan went the next morning and found Pepper washed up on shore. It was the only time I've seen him cry."

The weight of it all hit me in waves.

"Why tell me now?" I asked.

"Because you're a part of it now," Leigh said. "And because Albert is watching you. He mimics everything you do. You're teaching him how to embrace it and how to use it."

I looked toward the hallway where Albert

slept.

"I didn't ask for this."

"None of us did," she replied, "but that doesn't mean we're not the right ones for the job."

The house settled softly around us; outside, the wind carried the sound of the ocean, while inside, everything else was becoming more complicated.

And then Leigh said something that changed everything.

"Scott, Albert doesn't age or weaken when he heals."

20.

Stan didn't stir for several days. He hovered somewhere between this world and the next, murmuring names no one in the room recognized and outstretching his hands to apparitions.

Leigh sat beside him and sang. Sometimes Albert would hold his hand and whisper,

"Wake up, Lolo. Just a little longer."

But mostly, the house was silent.

When he opened his eyes one morning, it was right before dawn. The sky was still bruised with shadows; the ocean was painted in charcoal and pearl. I heard Stan stirring and I rose from the couch and went to him, and for a moment, he looked confused.

"You came back," he said.

"To be honest, I never left."

"Good," he coughed, tried to sit up, and groaned. "Help me sit."

I propped him up with pillows, and he clutched my arm.

When he settled, his breath came easier.

"And Leigh?" he asked.

"We all spent the night; She's making tea."

"Tell her to bring the good kind. The green stuff I hide in the drawer she thinks I don't know she found."

I grinned.

"You always know everything?"

He looked at me, and in that brief flicker, I saw the true sharp but humble man he'd become. "No," he said. "But I've learned to pay attention."

Leigh came in a bit apprehensive, with Albert trailing behind her. She set down the cup and Albert climbed onto the bed beside Stan, who touched his cheek and whispered something into his ear. The boy nodded solemnly, then leaned into his father's side.

"I don't have much left," Stan said, glancing between the three of us. "I feel it draining faster now: the life, the light, and mostly, the need to stay here— it's time."

We didn't argue. The truth was staring us in the face.

"Take me to the ocean," he said.

"You're not strong enough," Leigh replied gently.

"I won't die in this bed," he said. "I won't die under a roof. I need the water; I want my feet in it."

We were quiet, though Leigh consented.

"We'll carry you."

Albert looked up.

"I'll help."

We waited until the tide was low and the sky was covered in pre-dawn wisps. Leigh wrapped Stan in a wool blanket, and I carried him with Albert and Leigh guiding each step. He weighed nothing; bone wrapped in clothing.

The bluff trail was soft beneath our feet and animals gathered around us as we ascended. Dogs, birds, and even the old three-legged cat that hadn't moved in weeks. They followed as if they understood.

At the water's edge, we placed the old wicker chair Stan used to keep on his back porch. We set it in the sand, right where the tide kissed the shore, and when we lowered him into it, he exhaled a sigh of relief.

"I remember the first time I dove off this coast." he said. "I wasn't looking for anything except a place to disappear."

Leigh knelt beside him, tears on her cheeks.

"I was cocky back then," he said, "arrogant and cold. I ruined lives, I Cut corners, and I played God without permission."

He coughed, and I offered water, but he waved it off.

"I thought I was helping until people started dying under my hands. They called me Dr. Death, and they weren't wrong. I worked void of feeling, like a machine rather than a man."

He looked toward the sky. His voice was hard to hear over the waves.

"Then I touched the light, and I felt what real human sacrifice was and what healing meant. Not fixing or patching up; real healing — a dance. The kind that takes from you, leaves you tired, less, and emptier but spiritually truer."

He closed his eyes.

"I healed a soldier who lost his leg in Kandahar, a little girl with no heartbeat for six minutes, and a woman with cancer so deep the bones had hollowed, and I took all of it: their pain, their wounds, and their fear. I paid in years, in organ decay, and memory."

Albert reached for his hand.

"But I also healed a liar who went back to lying and a thief who kept stealing. A man who beat his wife and an alcoholic with cirrhosis who immediately picked up the bottle again, and I wondered… was it worth it?"

He looked at us, so serious and sure of his next words.

"The answer is YES."

Leigh sobbed, and I turned away — my throat burned.

"I got to be useful," he said. "For a time, I got to make a difference."

His breaths came shorter but with less struggle. He'd stopped fighting for the air he needed.

"Tell them." He whispered. "Tell everyone who asks... that I gave what I could, that I tried to repair and make up for what I did, and that I loved more in the end than I ever thought possible."

He looked at me; no, he looked into me.

"Scott, you carry it now, and you will carry me."

I solemnly promised with two words.

"I will."

Stan smiled and looked down the beach.

"I see them," he said. "*I see them all.*"

"The ones I touched, the ones I failed. I see their faces, and I'm not afraid."

His voice faded, and I tilted my head closer to listen.

"The girl with the burned hands, the boy with the hole in his heart, and the old man with lungs full of ash. The dancer, the addict, the mother with twins inside her—I see them and I remember. Doesn't that count for something?"

As Stan listed the ones he'd failed and held so dear, I saw them too.

I saw them gathered just along the water's edge. I saw them, smiling, joyous in his return. As sure as I was standing there, so were they, and I was bewildered.

Leigh touched his chest and told him,

"You can let go."

He looked at the water, eyes glinting with salt and tears.

"Take me home; I want to go home now," he pleaded, sounding like a child.

And then, with one last breath — as if he'd waited for her permission — he was gone.

We stayed there a while, holding him as the waves came and went. The chair rocked gently with the tide, and when the sun shone above the horizon, we did as he'd asked and carried him into the Pacific, completely submerged into the only place that he ever felt he belonged.

For a moment, there was only the wind but then, the ocean began to glow. It started faint, like moonlight caught beneath the surface, but then came a shimmer, silver and luminous.

The water, calm moments before, had an ethereal glow. Tendrils of silvery mercury emerged and swirled gracefully around him. It rose from the depths, something humanoid and alive, like an octopus with all of its tentacles lovingly encircling the body of the man who had carried so many wounds that weren't his to bear. This was the very essence that had once granted him strength and purpose, relieving him of it.

Birds squawked overhead, fish jumped all around us and the ocean cast a radiant light into the early morning sky, as if acknowledging the return of its own. In that moment, it felt as though the universe had come full circle, embracing Stan in the same elemental force that had defined his journey from the beginning.

The water swallowed him gently, reverently, until it reclaimed him completely. The glow pulsed once more, brighter than before, and then vanished into the dark beneath us.

The thing that had given him his power had come to take him home, probably to the light, and, as we stood in the water, letting the magic of the moment play out, I had a thought.

Perhaps I'd seen a glimpse into my future, my own ending, and I wasn't unhappy with it. It brought me peace and resolution.

I bent down to hug Albert and Leigh.

There we were, with a beach full of animals, on our knees in the sand, with tear-streaked faces, loaning each other our strength. I scooped Albert up into my arms, and with Mozart safely tucked against my chest, I took Leigh's hand, and together we walked the trail back to our lives.

lives that would never be as whole as they had been before that day.

21.

The baby grand stood quiet in the great room, draped in a thin layer of dust and a pale blue cloth. Stan would have been mortified.

Morning sun filtered through the wide windowpanes, slanting across the keys and I stood before it longer than I meant to with my hand hovering over the cover. I don't know what pulled me toward it. Maybe it was the silence after Stan, maybe it was the ache that had nowhere else to go, or maybe it was just time. All I know is that it looked as lonely as I felt.

I lifted the cloth and folded it carefully, placing it over the nearby chair. The keys beneath were slightly yellowed but whole and familiar, and my fingers relaxed as they settled into position.

I didn't warm up or test a scale; I just started playing.

The notes came hesitant at first, like a voice that was not quite sure it remembered the song, and then they gathered smooth and sorrowful. The piece was *"Spiegel im Spiegel"* by Arvo Pärt—simple, repetitive, and haunting, with each note a ripple across water.

I didn't plan it; I hadn't played it since the girls were little. It used to be their lullaby; it would remain theirs, and maybe that's why I needed to hear it.

The piano filled the room—soft, fragile, and mournful.

When I finished, I kept my fingers on the keys a moment longer, letting the final note fade, and it was only then that I heard her.

Leigh stood in the doorway, one hand over her heart, the other bracing the frame like she wasn't sure if she should come closer or leave me in peace.

"I didn't mean to intrude," she said.

"You weren't."

Her voice was strained. "That was beautiful."

"It was a lullaby," I said, "for my daughters.

Sarah used to say it could stop a war."

Leigh came over, her bare feet silent against the slick floor, and sat beside me on the piano bench. Her presence never intruded; it just *was.*

"I haven't really played a piano in years," I said.

"Could've fooled me."

I moaned and turned red, a bit embarrassed knowing that the last few days I had stolen a moment or two to touch the piano, even if I hadn't given into it. Playing had always been a mainstay in my life, and it brought me comfort even on the worst days.

I looked at her then, really looked. The way her eyes expressed warmth, the faint smile she always wore and the way grief and grace lived in her face at the same time.

She was beautiful. Not only in the physical way but also in the enduring way. In the *"I've survived too, and I'm still here"* way.

And suddenly, in that moment, everything was made clearer to me.

"I think I belong here," I said. "With you and Albert. I don't know how to explain it... it's not about filling a gap or trying to replace something I won't ever be able to; it's that when I'm with you both, I don't feel lost."

In an instant, Leigh's eyes changed mood and became filled with hope.

"You do belong here," she whispered. "You came because you were called. Not by Stan, but by the ache in your own chest, and that's how the best ones come."

I looked back at the keys and ran a single finger across them.

"Albert's been watching you," she added. "Mimicking you. He asked me yesterday if he could learn piano."

I chuckled. "He's got enough talents."

"He wants to be like you."

That weight, so heavy but also so welcome, settled across my shoulders.

"You're a part of his story now," Leigh said.

I turned toward her. "And what about your story?"

She answered, not coy or uncertain, but honest.

"I've spent a long time writing it alone;

maybe it's time to let someone else hold the pen."

I took her hand.

And for the first time in years, my heart didn't ache as it opened.

***

That evening, the fire crackled low in Leigh's hearth, licking around the base of the last log. The house still smelled like dinner, and Leigh was tucking Albert into bed. I stood alone in the kitchen; my hands wrapped around a chipped mug of chamomile. I felt full in a way I hadn't in years and still, somewhat hollow.

She returned and sat across from me. Her hair was loose, her knees drawn up into the chair, with her arms wrapped around them like a teenager.

"I think it's time I tell you about my girls," I said.

She didn't speak but patiently waited to give me time and space to gather my thoughts, like she'd known the moment was coming.

"My wife's name was Sarah and we met at a

diner. Nothing special about that spot, except for the pie. She said I looked like a man who ate too much pie, and I asked her what kind of girl counts another man's slices… I think I'd heard that line in a movie once, and it worked. That was our first conversation, and we were married three years later."

I smiled into my tea.

"We had two daughters, Hope and Rebecca. With blond curls and blue eyes — they looked like their mother. Loud, stubborn, and brilliant, they made everything in me wake up. They made me a better man; I know that now."

Leigh leaned in, resting her chin on the back of her hand.

"There was a storm the night they died, and I don't remember much before the phone call. I Just remember the rain, and a police officer who didn't know how to tell me gently."

I paused; the words felt stuck in my throat.

"Drunk driver. Sarah was driving them home from ballet, and they never made it. I lost them all."

Leigh's eyes welled, but she held back the

tears.

"I walked around for months like I was in a bubble. Mornings were the worst. Waking up and remembering. That's when I started painting and writing again, and even though I told myself it was for work, it wasn't. I think I was trying to resurrect them word by word. Writing about them kept them alive, and it worked for a while."

Overcome with emotion, I wept as I explained it all to her.

"That's why I believed you, and that's why I stayed. Because once you lose everything, the only thing that makes any sense is the extraordinary."

She came around the table and sat beside me. She didn't touch me at first but leaned in close and put her head on my shoulder, and when her fingers finally found mine, I was relieved.

"You carry it like it's made of glass," she said.

"I think I'm still afraid of dropping it."

I didn't pull her into me like I so desperately wanted to, and I still don't know why.

22.

It took some time for me to settle in. I had no desire to return to my old life and figured with what I had put away in my 401(k), I would be fine.

I was always frugal, especially since I became a widower, and never really did anything with the life insurance policies for Sarah and the girls. Donna helped me rent out my modest home in the suburbs and it sealed the deal. There was no longer a reason to go back to the job, the home, or the past.

Instead, I threw myself into living and learning how to be present; something I saw as a necessary attribute for anyone in my position. But mostly, I focused on little Albert.

After a few months of instructing him, I realized he was way out of my league. He was, by all accounts, a mathematical genius. Gifted — and not just in algebraic equations. It was astounding what he knew in all aspects of math, to include trigonometry, geometry, and algebraic methods I'd never even heard of. He adored astronomy, geology, geography, history, and physics. But chemistry—chemistry was his main obsession.

I took one of my visitors to Stan's house. It had become a habit, really; that space felt so powerful when I used my abilities, as if I wasn't alone. I derived strength from my brother's space. His smell and his essence seemed to sit in on our sessions.

The sentence I just wrote came so easily that after it was written, I had to pause and read it again—a few times.

"I derived strength from my brother."

I had a brother... I barely had time to get used to the idea, and as much as that hurts, I will continue.

I led the man into the study that day, and before we started, he had a lot to say.

He was a young one, around twenty-nine, I'm guessing and before I even knew his name or issue, he was against Stan's wall, running his hands down the spines of books I had only skimmed the surface of. His name was Patrick, and he was a college professor. He took one of the books off of the shelf with such excitement it was infectious.

I would learn that the book he held was a very rare 1st edition, but not only that one; *most* of the collection was.

His joy was palpable. So, I let him speak on things he loved for a while before we got down to the brass tacks of the visit.

He was self-soothing, and I let him.

When he finally told me why he'd come, it caught me off guard. He had a tumor in his frontal lobe. A diagnosis he'd gotten the month before. He didn't want to stop his research or teaching; it was the only thing he ever loved. Afraid that surgeries, radiation, and the normal cancer treatment would leave his mind and body too frail or ignorant to continue, he chose to see me *first*.

It was highly unusual. From my experience thus far, I'd learned that I was normally the *last* stop for anyone in his situation, never the first.

The session went very well, and I knew he was going to be okay. I walked him to the gate and invited him to come back any time he would like to use the books. I was hoping to learn enough to catch up with Albert so I could teach him properly, but that didn't happen. Well, it did, but in a different way.

After Patrick left, I went back to the office. I knew I was going to be sick but I didn't know to what extent, and I preferred to keep Albert from seeing me that way.

That time wasn't too bad, and when I opened my eyes later that night, I ate the food Leigh left for me. Then my mind wandered straight to the perfect, private library I had barely considered since the first day I'd met Stan.

I stood in front of the shelves briefly before choosing one. It wasn't bigger or smaller, shorter, or taller than the others; it's just the first one I chose.

I sat down in the leather chair behind the desk and turned the light on to investigate the volume that felt so very heavy and too smart, even before I knew its contents.

Theology. The book was a theology book entitled "Of Grammatology" by Jacques Derrida. I began to read with little expectation and finished it by 10:00 am.

As I closed it, my mind raced. I wasn't tired, but instead, I was exhilarated and fascinated, and I didn't want to stop. I stood, stretched, grabbed some water, and reached for another.

The next one was about the Trachtenberg method, a speed system of basic mathematics that I finished rather quickly, which wasn't the surprising part. Not only had I finished it, but I was also able to understand, apply, and master the method before dinnertime.

My comprehension was beyond anything I had ever experienced or could have imagined.

With the initial confusion of it all, I realized it must be part of the gift, and after careful consideration, it made sense.

My need to learn became insatiable.

I didn't sleep that night either; I didn't even think about sleep. There was something electric in me, like a charge had been lit in my brain that

I couldn't quiet down. That first book had opened a door, and the second had blown it off the hinges.

I kept reading. My fingers found book after book — titles I'd always considered too dense, too complicated, or too academic to bother with. Political theory, molecular biology, Jungian analysis, advanced calculus, ancient Sumerian texts — anything I reached for seemed to spill itself into me like it had been waiting.

By morning, I'd read four books and understood them completely.

The comprehension wasn't surface-level either. I could quote passages, summarize theories, apply formulas, and explain the material like I'd been studying it for years. At first, I thought it was a fluke, a one-time side effect of the healing, but by day three, I stopped questioning it.

It wasn't normal, and it wasn't temporary, so I started keeping another notebook.

At least, I called it that. It ended up more like a personal encyclopedia where I wrote everything I absorbed. Not out of fear that I'd forget, but because the act of writing became as effortless and satisfying as the reading. My handwriting changed too—it got tighter, cleaner, and almost calligraphic, as if my fingers had a mind of their own or belonged to someone else entirely.

Leigh noticed I wasn't around as much during the day. I still helped Albert in the mornings and made time for meals, but otherwise, I was in Stan's study every spare second.

When Albert went to sleep at night, I stayed in that chair, devouring entire volumes under a single lamp until the morning birds sang.

At some point, Leigh poked her head in and said,

"Be careful you don't burn out."

I smiled but didn't answer, because I wasn't burning out; I was burning brighter.

23.

The first time I realized that I could read a page in under a second, I laughed aloud. I timed it, over and over again. My eyes crossed the text like a film reel, a rush of symbols and meaning flooding in — and it seeded. It *stuck.* Every word and every nuance, as if I'd written it myself.

Speed reading wasn't just a skill anymore; it was instinct.

I began to sort books by subject matter, depth, and complexity. I wasn't just reading; I was absorbing entire disciplines, and by the end of that week, I had read ninety-seven books cover to cover. Some were small, yes, but many weren't, and I didn't skim; I mastered.

One afternoon, I read a linguistics primer in Portuguese. I hadn't known Portuguese, but after two books, I understood it; after four, I could think in it; by the tenth, I could speak it aloud, fluently and with the accent of someone who had lived in São Paulo his whole life.

Then came French, Russian, and Farsi. I didn't study them; I simply read and my brain did the rest. I could speak to Leigh in Tagalog, like I'd been born in the Philippines. She was shocked!

By week two, I was teaching Albert again, but it was different because I had no notes and no hesitation. I could see where his young mind was headed, and I met him there. Sometimes one step ahead; sometimes many.

He loved it and challenged me. He brought puzzles and theories and debates to breakfast like they were comic books. We'd go for walks, and he'd quiz me on chemical bonds or Egyptian astronomy and I never failed. It thrilled him and humbled me.

Because despite all I was becoming, Albert was still the most original thinker I'd ever met. The boy didn't just *know* things; he *saw* through them. While I was becoming a well-fed machine, he remained something rarer — an intuitive prodigy. I admired him more each day.

Still, the knowledge kept coming.

I learned carpentry from blueprints, chemistry from medical journals, and even sculpture from a set of dusty monographs left untouched on Stan's bottom shelf. I didn't just learn them; I practiced. I began carving, building, mixing, and testing. Everything I read begged for expression, and I couldn't help myself.

One night, I dreamed entirely in Mandarin, and when I woke, I wrote an essay in it.

The next morning, Leigh found me in the study again, still at the desk and I'd scribbled notes in six different alphabets. She scanned my desk when she first walked in, holding a cup of tea.

"Scott," she said, setting the cup down, "are you alright?"

I looked up at her, bleary-eyed but tingling with mental light.

"I think so; I feel as though I'm leveling up," I said. "Like I'm catching up on a lifetime of not knowing."

She smiled then.

"Please don't forget to live while you're learning."

I heard her and she made sense, but I didn't answer her because *I wasn't sure I could stop*.

***

That evening, I took the journal of Stan's out of the drawer and thumbed through it.

In the middle of one of the pages, a name caught my attention. *Martin Morris*. I paused, then continued reading the other pages, but my mind kept going back to that name. I sought it out again and again. Simple entry: Martin Morris, "no-show." There was no other information, but somewhere in the file cabinet of names that I was sure that I knew, that one was screaming.

Before I went in for supper, I remembered why.

Martin Morris was on my first birth certificate, before I was adopted; it was my biological father's name. It hung with me for several days, but I felt the pull and wondered if he would show up.

I was definitely not going to go searching for him—even if he was sick…or maybe it was the *different pull* Stan spoke of. Either way, I made up my mind that he would have to come to me.

That day came a few weeks later.

24.

My thirst for knowledge continued; the healing work continued, and Albert and I became synced in a way I cannot explain. My care for Leigh deepened and developed as any relationship that is *meant to be* can, and will, if given the proper time and space.

We began a life. Not like the ones that burn fast and fizzle out, but the sort that builds like a quiet tide, one ripple at a time, based on respect, honesty, kindness, and the knowledge that we held a secret — all three of us.

I'd wake up early and make coffee the way she liked it: dark roast with a splash of cream and no sugar. She'd smile at the gesture but say nothing, and I appreciated that about her. There was so much joy in the small, simple acts of daily devotion.

Albert devoured book after book. When I finished one, I passed it down to him, and it felt as if we were somehow sponging off one another's abilities. With what he was born with, what he'd learned from Stan and what we were passing between us, he was a little superhuman.

I'd catch him reciting facts in languages I didn't even know he knew: Italian, French, and Arabic, among others. He didn't simply read anymore; he, too, retained and applied.

I'd watch him build small contraptions out of scrap metal in the shed, test circuits, and sketch equations on the large chalkboard on the wall in his room like a little Da Vinci. It didn't feel like I was raising him anymore; it felt like I was witnessing the unfolding of something rare, something placed here with intention.

And the people, they kept coming.

More and more names were filling up Stan's old ledger. Every couple of weeks I would have a new entry to record or see one he hadn't had the chance to heal in his lifetime. I no longer questioned how I received them; it didn't matter. They came to me randomly when I was awake and at times in my dreams, and I accepted and recorded them.

There was a current moving through it all, and I was learning to trust it.

Some days I'd come home exhausted, the sort of exhaustion that affected me body and soul, and more times than not, I'd be sick.

But Leigh would be there, on the porch or inside cooking, with her hair tied up and a record playing low in the background and it soothed my soul.

She never asked what happened during a healing session unless I wanted to share. She understood the weight of it and respected the silence it often left behind.

One evening, we took Albert to the beach. He ran ahead while we walked hand in hand.

"I think he's different," she said, watching him draw equations into the sand with a stick.

"He is," I said.

"You too, you know."

I turned to her. "Different how?"

"Like you're finally becoming who you were supposed to be—not only a healer or the man who lost everything, but so much more."

Her words affected me in a way I can't

explain. I hadn't felt whole in a long time, and maybe she was right; maybe grief doesn't end; maybe it simply evolves into something else. Something like a quieter life, a deeper love, or a second chance that I just needed to embrace.

Later that night, when Albert had gone to bed, Leigh and I sat outside with glasses of red wine. The stars twinkled above us, and the ocean roared with each rolling in of the tide.

"I used to think I'd be alone forever," she said. "Not in a sad way, but I had accepted it."

"Me too."

She looked at me then, like she was still trying to figure me out even after all of the time we'd spent in each other's company.

"You know, you don't have to be perfect," she said. "You just have to stay."

I pulled her close to me, because I knew exactly what she meant, and I had no intention of going anywhere.

I didn't know where the road ahead led; more names would come, and more people would show up in their perfect timing. More healing, and possibly more sacrifice on my part, but for then, in that quiet sliver of time, I allowed myself to simply exist with her and Albert, and with a version of myself I never thought I'd meet again.

***

It was a sunny day in July when a man stepped through the front gate and I didn't have to ask who he was. I knew it was Martin Morris.

He looked to be an older, worn version of me.

I'd seen the name in Stan's journal weeks earlier, and I turned the page as if the name meant nothing, but it meant everything. He was my biological father. I hadn't seen him since I was a little boy, and even then, it was only in fragments. My memories of him were more like apparitions than recollections.

We were having a small birthday party for Albert that day. It was Leigh, Donna, her kids, her sister, a couple of neighbors, a string of balloons, and a homemade cake with too many sprinkles. Albert was beaming, and the day was perfect and easy, **until it wasn't.**

Martin didn't come for healing, even though I smelled it. Whatever it was, it was advanced. One of my new talents: I could *smell* something no one else could — *illness*.

No, he hadn't come for a reunion or relief; he'd come for judgment.

He was lean and weathered, with eyes sharp beneath a brow that had seen too many years of pride and too few of real grace or understanding. His Bible was tucked beneath his arm and he didn't even introduce himself or say hello; he just assumed I knew, and I still find that weird.

"Scott," he said, as if saying my name gave him grief. "I've heard stories that you're healing people."

I gave a cautious nod.

"I try to help."

He stepped closer, lowering his voice.

"Help? Son, let's not play games. This power... this thing you're doing. If it's not from the Lord, it's from the enemy, you know that."

"I never claimed..."

"But you haven't denied it either," he cut in.

"You give no glory to Jesus Christ, and that's all I needed to hear."

He opened his worn Bible; the margins overflowed with notes.

"Let me read you something."

His voice rose slightly, not enough to alarm the children nearby, but enough to make me reposition myself between him and our guests.

"And no marvel; for Satan himself is transformed into an angel of light. Therefore, it is no great thing if his ministers also be transformed as the ministers of righteousness.'"

His eyes burned as he closed the book.

"Second Corinthians, chapter eleven. You understand what that means?"

I held his gaze.

"It means you've already made up your mind."

He looked around the yard, at Albert laughing with frosting on his nose, at Leigh setting out paper plates, and at the calm joy of a life I had only recently begun to believe I deserved.

"I came to give you a chance, son. To come

back to the truth and to give the glory to God before it's too late."

I didn't answer. Not right away. I felt the old weight return—the desire to be seen, to be accepted, and to be claimed by someone who had left too long ago—but I also felt something else. I felt the steady root of my own becoming, and in that moment, I gave silent thanks to the powers that be that gave me my adoptive parents.

"You came on a child's birthday to argue ownership of a gift you don't understand," I finally said. "That's not the kind of God I believe in. Are we done here?"

He stared at me for a bit and then shook his head.

"You'll see one day; you'll know what spirit you've entertained."

He turned, walked out of the gate, and started down the steps without looking back.

25.

On a beautiful, hot day in August, Leigh and I were married.

A small affair, with our gazebo draped in soft linen and late summer flowers tucked inside organza along the edges of the bent-branch archway. Wildflowers were in jars on tables and in Leigh's bouquet, and the guest list fit at a single table: Donna and her kids, a few neighbors, and the justice of the peace. That was it. There was no spectacle or staged photographs; it was just us, saying what we already knew.

We didn't need a wedding to prove we were committed but it felt right to claim one another out loud. To mark the day we became a family, not only in spirit, but by law.

Obtaining the license was mildly amusing. The clerk raised an eyebrow, skeptically tapping Leigh's ID once, then again.

Leigh smirked, like she'd answered questions too many times in too many ways, and said,

"Paperwork's right; biology's another story."

The woman nodded slowly, unconvinced but too polite to say more, and we left with a signed form and a laugh. Albert skipped between us, carrying a small bag of birdseed he insisted we toss instead of rice.

I stood under that gazebo with Albert by my side, his chest puffed out like a best man twice his age, while Mozart hopped happily around our feet.

Leigh walked toward us in a pale blue dress, her hair pinned back with something borrowed and Donna, aided by a cane, walked beside her, holding her bouquet and wiping at her eyes before she even reached us.

I've seen beauty in many forms: sunrises on boats, deep ocean light, and the raw brilliance of healing someone on the edge, but nothing held a candle to my fiancé. Not because of the dress or the way the sun caught her hair, but because of what we had built quietly — day by day, moment by moment.

We had fallen in the same way ivy grows: slowly, persistently, wrapping around each other until one could not be removed without tearing the other apart. Strangely enough, we arrived at that point of being completely in love without physical intimacy to guide or distract us. We had gotten to know each other on a level that most people skip.

After the cake was cut and the gazebo had emptied, we walked home together, with our hands held tight and our boy beside us tugging the leashes of two mutts too excited to behave.

That night, after Albert was asleep and the house was quiet, we met again. Not only as friends, caretakers, and companions, but as man and wife; as lovers.

It was soft and clumsy, almost to the point of being comical. But it was real and beautiful.

And when I woke in the middle of the night with Leigh's head resting on my chest and the moonlight falling across our tangled feet, I knew without question that I was where I belonged.

***

Morning sun poured through the windows like honey, warm and golden, touching every surface with soft light. I awoke to the sound of birds outside and for once, I wasn't in a rush. With no pressure to figure out the next move, no calls for healing, and no looming questions about purpose or fate. Just the normal sounds that come with a new day, to include a very excited rooster.

Leigh was already up, her robe tied loosely around her waist as she moved about the kitchen, barefoot, and singing. The smell of cinnamon and coffee lured me in like a magnet. I stepped over and wrapped my arms around her waist. She leaned back into me without saying a word, her body fitting perfectly against mine. We stayed like that, enjoying our togetherness.

"You're not working today?" She asked, smiling as she handed me a cup.

"No one's dying, no one's crying, and no one's calling; I think today is ours."

She raised her mug to mine.

"To ours."

As our cups clinked, Albert came thudding down the stairs, still in his pajamas, hair sticking up like a wild crown.

"Do I smell cinnamon rolls?"

Leigh laughed, pulling a tray from the oven.

"Made fresh, genius boy."

The three of us ate on the back porch, passing napkins and licking icing from our fingers. The air was sweet with blooming Gardenias, bees hovered over the flowerbeds, and the world didn't feel broken. It felt like something worth being a part of.

After breakfast, we packed a picnic basket. Leigh made sandwiches and fruit salad, and Albert insisted we bring chess and the old radio he'd fixed. We drove to the park with the big oak tree close to town. Albert ran ahead, climbing everything he could, laughing freely, his feet barely touching the ground.

"He's growing so fast," Leigh said as we spread the blanket.

"And into something remarkable," I added.

She sat down and opened the picnic basket.

"It's strange. I don't know how we got here, but I love this, and I would never want to go back to anything else."

"We're not going back," I said. "Only forward."

We lay there for hours. I read while Leigh dozed beside me, with her head on my chest. Albert beat me twice at chess and then wandered off with a sketchpad, drawing the ducks in the pond with serious concentration.

Around us, life went on—kites in the sky, children playing tag, and the occasional bark of a happy dog—but inside our little circle, there was peace.

Late in the afternoon, the breeze blew cooler, and Leigh and I danced barefoot in the grass to an old Sam Cooke song.

I had a family again, and I couldn't take my eyes off of them.

26.

In the span of a year, I helped one hundred and thirty-six people.

I was suffering. Not all of the time, but certainly more than I was prepared for.

What I've learned is that I don't just heal them; I seem to acquire the illness myself, if only for a while. It lingers — the pain, the fear, the sickness — it manifests inside of me. When someone is in the end stages of whatever affliction they have, it takes me days or even weeks to feel healthy again.

Each time it becomes more difficult for me, even though the healing process itself has become simpler. The mental gymnastics I used to get myself through the rough bouts, to try to change things, to plan a way for my journey to end differently than Stan's — well, it seemed futile.

I had all but accepted it was the way it was

supposed to be.

But you see, it became out of the question to let it go. Leigh, to our surprise and delight, was pregnant, and I couldn't give up and let things play out.

It was then that we developed a solid set of ground rules, based on Stan's habits he'd only discussed briefly with Leigh and not at all with me.

Let me explain.

When I took his place as the repairman, there was still much I did not understand. I was learning as I went, following intuition with the people I mended.

I began spending more time in bed recuperating than I was raising Albert or being a proper husband to Leigh, and I knew I couldn't go on that way. I had to find balance.

So, we took steps to slow things down.

I was already showing signs of aging in small, undeniable ways, and I wanted to be around to raise Albert as well as our unborn child.

The rules Leigh remembered were for our

own protection and peace, and the most obvious one was to fly below the radar. So, we had to start seeing those in need by appointment. We all agreed to try and keep the healing going on at the ridge a secret and to tell nobody where the power came from. We didn't need thousands of divers converging on the water below in search of it, and I was concerned about any media attention. I didn't want to be the subject for scientists to study or the reason the police felt the need to intrude.

Word of mouth is powerful, and for a while, we had to turn people away as I went strictly from the names that came to me. (That was the worst feeling ever.) Also, anyone I healed had to fit into an age range that wouldn't be suspicious, or they would change and agree to relocate, like Leigh had done.

Infants, children, pre-teens, teenagers, and people in their twenties, thirties, or forties were excellent candidates. Their side effects, other than being healthy overnight, were not that drastic. Not like someone in their fifties, sixties, or seventies. Leigh was a great example; she'd returned to the healthiest point in her life, which was around twenty-seven. From there, she would continue to age at a normal rate.

I couldn't afford to be lazy and many times went to find the people on the list to keep the traffic from our place and to protect our privacy— and on that list was Donna.

The day finally came that the pull was too strong to ignore, and I knew she was in trouble.

Leigh, Albert, Mozart, and I loaded up in the car and headed to her house in the pouring rain. Of all the pain I'd felt, hers was the worst.

Not because of her disease; multiple sclerosis was curable and simple enough. She and Leigh had become quite close over the course of time, and she'd told her in confidence.

Leigh had also been very honest with Donna about everything. The process, the age regression, and the knowledge that she would essentially be starting over from where she was in her prime. We couldn't guarantee what age that might be.

Donna had been on my list since before the wedding, and when we left that evening in the rain, I knew it was then or never.

She lived in an adobe Spanish-type home right outside of town, on a well-manicured, sleepy little street. I'd known her husband, William, since their second date, a nice, rather quiet man who drew much of his strength from Donna and their kids.

He was waiting on the porch when we arrived. Sunken, sleep-deprived, and worried. His eyes were bloodshot, and I am not sure if it was from crying or the sleepless nights. Probably both.

We greeted one another, shook off our rain gear, and left it dripping on the porch as we followed him in.

After the normal forced pleasantries, he spoke for a few minutes about where Donna was in terms of health, and in the middle, he broke down. He had his elbows on his knees, hands clasped in front of him, sobbing.

Leigh reached over and placed her hand on his.

"I know, William, it's okay; we are here to help."

That was always what my wife was good at: consoling, empathy, and compassion. I stood with my hands in my pockets while Albert observed. He watched every single interaction as if taking mental notes.

Leigh popped into the kitchen to put on fresh coffee, and I was left to calm him enough to direct me to Donna. I knew in my gut it had to happen quickly; I could feel it in their house that death was about to win. I was afraid I'd waited too late, and there was no time to lose.

We went to the dining room a few feet from where we stood. The door swung inward, and I saw something that caught me off guard.

The space had been transformed into a hospice room. Hospital bed, aids to help her sit up or to go to the bathroom, and she had a feeding tube in since she'd lost the ability to swallow. A wheelchair sat in the corner, and when I saw her, I hardly recognized the frail, skinny woman she'd become. Her hands were drawn up to her chest, in what we refer to as the t-rex position: wrists bent inward, fingers pulled tightly together.

I went to her, but before I could lay hands on the one that I loved, I was stopped.

lying on the table beside her bed, there was a letter with my name on it. I opened it and read the words—words I think I already knew were coming.

Scott,

I need you to understand that as hard as this is, as awful as it sounds to you now, I know you will eventually agree. We are family, you and I. You have been a brother to me, an uncle to my kids and a wonderful friend and work companion. But, as much as I do not want to die now, I can't and will never make a choice that will allow me to be healthy and alive while I watch the people I love die before me. I couldn't bear it. To be given a new, younger body isn't what I want. I have had a wonderful life, and I do not want to have a do-over for something I got perfectly right the first time around. To leave William behind, I must do, but to live without him in this world, or possibly outlive my children, I JUST CAN'T and I WON'T. Please understand. Your gift is a spectacular display of selfless love, but it is not for me. Please, let me go. It is truly my final wish. I am so glad to have witnessed your evolution into a happy family man again, with purpose.

Love, Donna

When I finished, her eyes were open. She'd watched me read her note. I put the letter in my pocket with the full weight of her wishes, and I knew I had to respect them.

And so, Leigh, Albert, and I said our goodbyes.

She heard us and she understood. We hugged her, and we talked to her for a while even though she was incapable of responding.

We spoke to her of the joy and laughter she created wherever she went. We spoke to her about all relevant topics, including the impact she had on our lives and others, as well as sharing our fondest memories. We spoke to her with honesty, knowing it would be the last time, and as we left the room, we each told her how much we would miss her.

Albert was the last to leave her side. He leaned toward her and whispered in her ear that the next life would be even better than this one. He told her he loved her and kissed her on the cheek.

A river of tears rolled from her eyes as we turned to go.

Later that night, surrounded by the people who meant the most to her, she went to sleep for the last time.

Yes, watching someone I considered family deteriorate and having the ability to save them but not having permission to do so was a next level of hurt. That day, I discovered a pain I had never known before. People like Donna are rare, and I guess I'm selfish; I wanted her to stay.

27.

The months that followed were strange without her; we all grieved the loss, and it did something unexpected to me.

I'd learned a valuable lesson.

Contrary to popular belief, if given the choice, I believe that many people would decline it just as Donna did, which led me to question my work entirely. Maybe I was tampering with something I shouldn't be.

If that were true, then the world was really just a constant survival of the fittest, and therefore life seemed more scientific. If our existence is ruled not by love or even fate and is solely dependent on the natural human order of things, isn't that the definition of natural selection?

If fate *were real*, and I changed things as important as life or death, would that in fact have a ripple effect?

For example, If I healed a sick man who was supposed to die so that his widow could meet her soulmate or have a child that was meant to be born with another, and that child was supposed to give something extraordinary to the world... then was my curing actually serving a good purpose in the grand scheme of things, or the exact opposite? I struggled to come to grips with the integrity of my assignment on this planet.

I couldn't decide. I only knew that I had to keep doing it, but with so much recently acquired knowledge and information swirling about in my head, of course I had to consider it.

***

Rules had to stay in place, and things seemed to get better. No heavy traffic and more time spent on studies, helping Leigh, and preparing for our new arrival.

I took Leigh into town one day to do some shopping for the baby. We chose a home birth because she wanted it, but also so no suspicion would be raised at the hospital — a hospital that already knew of her illness, background, and age. She'd done the same with Albert to remain *under the radar.*

Stan had been a doctor, and I wasn't, so it was very frightening for me, even after I delved into every single medical textbook I could get my hands on concerning labor and delivery. I paid special attention to things that could go wrong, but I still felt extremely unprepared.

Anyway, that day we left Albert at home with his homework and planned to be gone around three hours.

*This next part of our story was dictated to me so that I may record and recount it, but it was Albert's experience, and it deserves to be heard.

After Leigh and I left for town, Albert was doing homework on the porch when people came to the gate.

A family. A man still in his work shirt and tie, his wife, a very pretty blond, and a little girl about the same age as Albert, with blue eyes and pale skin. She wore a knee-length yellow dress with a matching bow around her hairless head.

Albert greeted them, and even though he knew the rules, he took one look at the little girl and welcomed them in. He told them his parents were gone, but he invited them to wait.

He took the girl named Paige by the hand, and with her parents' permission, he led her to the rabbit hutches. Of course, Mozart wasn't caged, and she was intrigued.

Albert picked him up and let her pet him, and she smiled a tired — final stage cancer smile, but when Albert put Mozart in her arms, her face still lit up. She stood with him, burying her nose into the top of the soft fur on his head.

Albert opened the rabbit enclosure to show her the newest litter, all white, with floppy ears and red eyes. She let out an excited giggle. He told her,

"You can have one if you want."

Paige pondered on the offer for a minute before saying,

"I can't; I am going to die and I won't be around to take care of it."

Her parents were standing close, and ever hopeful, she looked to them. The mother immediately answered,

"Please, don't say that, Paige; you will get better."

The father looked at his wife, turned his head to the side, and said something about false hope.

"It isn't healthy or helpful, Jane."

Paige cuddled the bunny to her chest and looked at them, eyes pleading.

Jane looked at her husband and whispered, "If there is no hope, then what does it matter? At least she has this."

He thought about it for a minute, reached over to stroke the animal in his daughter's arms, and gave in.

"We will take one. How much do we owe you?"

"Oh, no sir, this is a gift! Let me get some rabbit pellets, a water dispenser, and a small carrier."

After he'd gathered supplies and explained everything they needed to know about caring for the little bunny, they were all set. At that point, he confessed to them that healing without an appointment wasn't possible. Seeing their grief and disappointment was too much for Albert.

The father handed him a business card and asked for Scott to call him.

He watched as they headed back to the gate with their new pet. Paige was trailing behind them and the pull to her became too much. He called out her name as he ran in her direction.

"Would you mind if I gave you a hug?"

Paige didn't even look at her parents for approval. She willingly threw her arms around Albert in a long, tight embrace.

Albert locked his arms around her tiny frame and rubbed his warm hands across her back and spine, and then pulled her in tighter until her head was on his shoulder, and he was able to place a hand on the nape of her neck and skull.

After a few minutes, she let out a breath of ease, and he released her.

She walked back to her parents, looking over her shoulder at Albert as she made her way down the steps. She stopped for one final wave before they disappeared.

Albert stood and rubbed his hands together.

He felt the exchange. He had healed his first human, and he knew it wouldn't be his last.

***

A few weeks later, Albert saw her name in Stan's journal, and he had no choice but to tell me what transpired that day. He apologized for it and gave me the business card.

After a quick call to inquire about Paige's health, it was confirmed that she was cancer-free and getting healthier each day. Her father said it was a *miracle*.

It seems that Albert was better than I was, for he suffered no side effects. It was amazing and a little scary.

And then, ***there were two repairmen.***

28.

A note from the Author

If you have made it this far, I need to admit a few things.

Firstly, writing doesn't come naturally to me. Writing about my life, as well as our shared experiences and losses, has been a colossal undertaking. So much change in such a short time would throw anyone into a tailspin. I know that now.

So, although I have tried to tell our story with as much detail as I can, I still have a family to protect.

The next part, the personal parts, the pieces of us that really challenged our belief systems and our sense of duty to do the right thing — in many areas — must be shared as well.

Leigh and I have to protect our children and our identities.

But in the end, I chose to share them, because

otherwise, you wouldn't have the complete picture.

Know that the chapters ahead were the most difficult to endure and almost impossible to put into words.

Please forgive me if I fail in relaying the most beautiful and surprising parts of our lives, as well as the most frightening.

Looking back, what happened, good and bad, didn't just teach us lessons; it strengthened and united us.

Scott

29.

It was three months after Donna's passing, and I cannot accurately describe how much I still missed her. Losing Stan and Donna, we'd lost our closest family members, and we felt their absence every day.

It was after midnight when Leigh nudged me awake, whispering my name. I could barely see her in the moonlight, but I heard the fear in her voice before I grasped her actual words.

"My water broke."

She was lying in a warm puddle, her hands calm but her eyes wide, and all I could think was, *not yet*. It was a month early. But then again, nothing about our life followed the calendar anymore.

I moved quickly, changing the sheets, helping her out of her clothes, and steadying her through the first waves of contractions. I'd read the books, annotated the margins, watched the videos and highlighted everything that could go wrong. But there's no amount of preparation that can truly ready a man for seeing the woman he loves caught between agony and creation.

In the end, the reality of it is that I stood on the sidelines and watched nature take its course. I was reduced to what every man becomes when put in that situation: a bundle of nerves and a silent cheerleader, stumbling over the simplest order. Thank God for Leigh's forethought.

She was composed in that way only she could be: quiet but fierce, wind-through-the-trees strong. She winced as a sharp contraction came, gripping my arm as she told me,

"Albert came so easily; this feels different."

I called the doula she'd kept on standby. A kind-eyed Filipino woman arrived in record time and introduced herself as Althea.

Leigh wanted her not for medical assurance but for comfort and that steady, feminine energy that knew how to anchor a woman in stormy waters.

Within an hour of her arrival, Leigh was almost fully dilated. By the third hour, the baby was crowning, giving us no time to pace and no time to question. Althea guided us through it like she'd done it a hundred times, and likely had.

Then he came.

Red-faced, lungs full of life, fists balled up like he was ready to take on the world. Leigh wept with exhaustion and joy, and I kissed her forehead again and again, repeating,

"You did it; you did so well."

But before I could even cut the cord, before we could bathe in the newness of it all, Leigh's face went pale, and her eyes widened.

"Something's wrong," she said. "I still need to push."

Althea's eyes lit up with experience, not panic. She examined Leigh, and I swear her arm was lost in Leigh up to her elbow when she gave a short laugh. Her face held disbelief laced with glee.

"There's another," she said, beaming. "You've got an extra; he must have been hiding."

My brain couldn't catch up... an extra *what*,

and *how*? In that small body, how could she have carried *two babies*? But I had no time to question it. Leigh was in the thick of it again, squeezing the side of the bed, her body begging for rest while she gave everything she had left to the hidden soul waiting to emerge.

Forty-five minutes later, she was here.

She was born so quiet and still. The type of stillness that takes your breath until the tiniest cry escapes. She opened her eyes wide and looked up at me. Time stopped, and I knew.

Not because a doctor said so, and not because she was tested or diagnosed. I recognized the slight curve of her eyes, the soft flat bridge of her nose, and the gentle shape of her short fingers. She had the unmistakable features of Down syndrome.

It didn't matter. I had our daughter in my arms, and none of it mattered. No fear, no questions, and no hesitation—only pride.

I held our beautiful girl against my chest, and she was perfect, because she was ours and she came from love. Because she was chosen, just like Albert, just like her brother now nestled in Leigh's arms.

Leigh looked at me, drained but radiant, and whispered,

"She's ours too, isn't she?"

I brushed a tear from her cheek with my thumb.

"Of course she is," I said. "Absolutely."

She grinned a weary, proud, sacred smile only a mother can give.

We named them quietly, together, in that moment. Thomas, for strength, and *Himala, for the *miracle she was.

Albert came in as the sun was rising, barefoot and rumpled from sleep. As he peeked around the door, he asked,

"Is it here?"

He crawled into bed beside Leigh, who was cradling his new siblings, eyes wide with wonder.

"Two...two babies?" he said in disbelief. He reached out to stroke their cheeks and touch their tiny fingers.

"They smell like warm bread, and I love them."

And then we were five.

Life, for all its storms, had made us the most complete family, and my heart felt as if it was going to burst out of my chest with pride.

30.

Things needed to change again on the ridge, if only temporarily. We all needed time to adjust and wanted to enjoy the babies.

We stayed up in our little haven for as long as we could. For Leigh to heal, and for me to be able to take part in all the things I'd missed with my girls in the past. I wanted to soak up every single second, and I chose to protect my new family at all costs.

It was our quiet time. Some of the best days of my life and I loved every minute of it.

After those six glorious months, things started to gradually ease back in. Stan was correct—you either heal or you slowly go mad.

But even after we started to let people past the gate that were on the list, or others that showed up that weren't, the way we took care of them changed.

Albert and I began to work together. He was

a child who had the mind and strength of a Mensa candidate. He was only lacking in experience and emotional development and that would come with time. I didn't want him to miss out on his childhood, but he was always pushing the envelope.

I — on the other hand — was a forty-two-year-old man who was starting to carry the same marks of the trade that Stan had.

Though my mind was strong, my body aged at a more rapid rate. My beautiful wife still looked to be quite young, and part of me wanted to stop healing so that I wouldn't miss my children growing up.

Stan made it to forty-seven. If I continued as he had, I would only see the twins reach their eighth birthday, if I were lucky. Which would leave Albert to help care of his mother and siblings.

I never had a moment's peace with it. It consumed my thoughts day and night, and yet, I couldn't quit either. I wouldn't go out as a martyr, and I was unsure how to solve it. It was a conundrum.

My children were all exquisite, from anyone's point of view.

Albert — appropriately named — was a little Einstein, but with abilities surpassing my own. Black thick hair, Stan's blue eyes, and a tall and slim physique that seemed to change overnight.

Thomas had dark hair, eyes that matched his mother's, and early mental development that I wasn't sure I should attribute to Albert's interest, or *obsession*, with teaching him, or his natural abilities. He was ahead in every single milestone and I knew, *we knew* from experience, it would just be a matter of time before the gift would show — or it wouldn't.

Himala was the jewel of the family and Leigh and the boys worshiped her. So did I. Slow to develop or hit any of the normal expectations, her sweet soul was enough to turn a dark day into a glorious one with just her presence. Her smile was so genuine, her hair so fair, and her skin so porcelain and light. She had all of my attributes, whereas Thomas had all of Leigh's.

Honestly, our children looked to be of all

different heritages; definitely not from the same family.

The love, the joy, and the light that we were a part of in our little corner of the world was something none of us ever wanted to end, and for a while, it felt possible to stay exactly the way we were.

Picnics on the beach, tending our garden, teaching our children, and loving each other were more than enough for all of us, and we were happy; truly happy.

We learned, we grew, we healed, and we aged. In the blink of an eye, the twins were four, and my body rapidly began to show life's toll. I no longer recognized myself in the mirror.

If I was doomed to the same fate Stan had, then I was living my last days. Leigh, Albert, and I knew it, but the twins didn't.

Himala was my welcome companion. She wanted to be with me, beside me, in my arms, or at least close enough to touch. She wasn't very verbal, but she was learning, and even though she had all of the telltale signs of Down syndrome, she also had an uncanny ability to read the room or understand when something wasn't said. Whether it was sadness, pain, anger, or frustration, her empathy was beyond anything I'd ever seen.

Albert started teaching her piano the year previous, and she wanted to be in front of the keys constantly. Her soft, stubby little fingers somehow bridged the gap between what she felt and couldn't verbalize. The music was her voice.

We all adored her, just the way she was.

At some point, Thomas started calling her Princess Himala, and she responded to him by calling him Prince-T, but for her it came out as one word, *Princetie*. We have no idea where the idea came from, but those two had a bond that I'm sure only twins can experience. It was fantastic to watch them interact. It was as if Thomas was her other half, often speaking for her when she didn't and knowing her desires or needs without being prompted. They truly were a part of one another.

So, when it was Himala who started to mold the next part of our lives, it came as not only a surprise but a complete shock. And that shock and inability to categorize her or see her as the rest of the world did would change our lives forever: Our direction, our methods, and our plans.

31.

It started with picket lines.

At first, it was just a few people scattered near the bottom of the ridge—holding signs, quoting scripture, and shouting ignorant things—but word spreads like wildfire when it's fanned by fear, and the man holding the largest sign was none other than Martin, my father.

His voice carried an unwanted sermon through the wind.

"False prophet!" he shouted. "Wolves in sheep's clothing!"

He quoted from Matthew, from Revelation, and from the parts of the Bible that people use when they want others to be scared. It seems that fear is, indeed, contagious.

He didn't come for healing; he came for a crusade.

I should have ignored it, but the others saw him too. Those we had helped, those on the list, and those quietly waiting to be seen. They started to pay attention and began to feel that if my own father, a preacher, stood against me, what did that say about the source of the gift?

So, we had a necessary family meeting.

Albert sat cross-legged on the rug, his expression serious beyond his years. Leigh stood near the window, swaying slightly with Himala in her arms, and Thomas, curious but unaware, played with a rubber ball near the couch. The weight in the room was real.

"I hate them," Albert said plainly. "I hate that they think we're evil."

"They're afraid," Leigh replied gently. "People get confused by what they don't understand."

"But we've helped so many," I said. "They know the difference we've made."

"Do they?" Leigh turned and stared at each of us.

"Do they *really* know? Or are they guessing, hoping, and believing from a distance? We've been private about it — too private. Maybe it's time we show them what it really looks like."

Albert's head jerked up.

"Like a documentary?"

"No," I said. "Like a session, a real session on camera for everyone to see exactly what we do and how we do it. To put their doubts to rest."

At first, the idea felt reckless, but the more we spoke about it, the more it made sense. We weren't charlatans, and this wasn't smoke and mirrors. What we did, what *I* did, was grounded in intention, presence, and compassion, and above all—love.

It was Leigh who made the final call when she said,

"We either hide and let the world decide who we are for us, or we show them the truth and let the truth stand on its own."

So, we arranged for a controlled group healing. Five people, chosen at random from past applicants, with a simple camera crew to record the process. No media circus, just one truth at a time.

Albert helped organize the logistics, drafted safety protocols, and insisted we publish a full list of ailments and consent forms online. He was eleven going on fifty.

The day of the recording, the sky was clear, and the temperature was tolerable. I wore plain clothes, and Leigh and the twins were present but seated to the side. Albert ran the audio, but otherwise it was us, like always.

One of the first to arrive — long before the lines grew long — was a local police officer named Reese Hammond; he didn't come in uniform. In fact, he came quietly, parking at the base of the road and walking up with a backpack slung over one shoulder.

Reese never demanded anything and didn't push his way forward. He simply asked if he could observe. He said he'd heard stories about Stan, about the bluff, and about the way people left feeling different, and when I agreed, he took a place in the back.

Reese would be a constant presence from that first group healing session until the last. It was reassuring for us to have an officer there.

We chose Stan's house for the space, and the group consisted of a woman with advanced

Parkinson's, a man with terminal lymphoma, a young veteran with chronic pain from an IED, a girl with recurring seizures, and a father who brought his nonverbal son.

I took them one by one, hand over hand, breath after breath, and it was grueling but good.

The energy in the room shifted, the same way it always did: with warmth, with receiving, and with a subtle tingle and tempo.

When it was over, there were tears. One of the crew members wept behind the camera as the girl with seizures hugged her mother without trembling, and the veteran sat up straighter than he had in years.

The footage was real. There was nothing over-dramatic, with no flashing lights or thunderbolts. It was Just healing and love...but it didn't stay beautiful for long.

At the end of the session, as people packed up, Leigh was rocking a very tired and cranky Himala gently in her arms, when someone noticed them and asked a question.

It came from behind a lens, quiet but sharp.

"What about her?"

Leigh looked up. "I'm sorry?"

"Your daughter. The one with…" The woman gestured vaguely, as if Down syndrome was too dirty to name. "Why hasn't *she* been healed?"

The room went still.

I stepped forward and answered for her.

"She's not sick."

"But she's *impaired*," the woman pressed. "You could fix her, couldn't you?"

"No," I said firmly. "Because there's nothing to fix."

A murmur swept through the crew. One man lowered his camera, and the energy in the room, once so full of hope, felt somewhat darker.

The same question spread across every face: *What sort of man heals strangers but won't heal **his own child**?*

But they didn't see what we saw. No one except for Reese.

In the midst of the chaos, he reached out and stroked Himala's cheek as if to agree with why the gift hadn't come for her. As if to remind himself that sometimes, not even miracles are a solution. There was no pity, only a deep understanding.

Himala wasn't broken. She wasn't dying; she was *thriving*. She brought music to the house, softness to our hearts, and balance to our minds. Her condition wasn't a defect; it was a blessing. She saw the world with pure eyes and a white heart.

But others didn't see that; they only saw what they didn't understand.

That night, after the house emptied and the children were asleep, I sat alone by the fire, turning the question over in my mind. I wasn't angry, just deeply, achingly tired.

Because in their eyes, I was a monster, not for who I'd healed, but for who I hadn't.

I grappled with that well into the night. Was it ethical for us to make a decision that would essentially have her dependent on us or others the rest of her life? I signed on to heal the sick, diseased and ones with accidental ailments, not a person's inherited chromosome make-up.

32.

After news of the healing session got out — and it did, with a quickness none of us could have imagined — we couldn't escape it.

The bottom of the ridge stayed full with reporters, the curious, and, of course, those who were ill. The police had to station an officer at the end of the walk near the old entrance to keep order. It was the end of our privacy.

Most of our food was grown, raised, or caught, but we still had to go into town periodically for necessities, and that became unbearable. People followed us, asked questions, and took pictures. We couldn't eat a meal or buy a bar of soap without someone interrupting.

So, we adapted again.

We decided that if we could let people in, maybe a group each week, we might retain some sense of normalcy. Small sessions from previous applicants or people on the list, carefully controlled.

And so, we set up the next group. This time, we held the session outdoors on the bluff behind the house, where the view overlooked the crashing surf below, and the gulls traced lazy circles above. It had rained the night before and the sky was still gray and threatening.

Something about that day felt off. It was uncommonly cooler than expected for late spring, but we'd already agreed to let one local news crew in, and we couldn't back out.

As the crowd gathered, the camera crews were already set up, running sound checks and installing lights. We'd marked off space in a wide circle. Five patients sat quietly in folding chairs: a woman in hospice care with stage four cancer who'd been carried all of the way up the steps by her son, a man with a leg brace and degenerative nerve damage, a teenage boy with Type I diabetes, and two others, chosen randomly from the growing list of requests.

Leigh watched from the porch, and Albert had positioned himself behind the small generator and camera monitors, directing the tech crew as if he owned the place.

As I was about to begin, in order from the youngest to the oldest, a commotion broke out at the gate.

I heard his voice before I saw him.

"He's a liar! *You're all being deceived!*"

I took the microphone from its stand. "Let him in," I told the officer. "But he stays silent, and if he interrupts again, he's to be removed."

Reese nodded and opened the gate. Martin walked through slowly, his face puckered with disapproval. He kept his distance, taking a place in the back of the crowd.

I turned my attention to the task at hand, took a breath, and began. In through the nose, out through the mouth.

The boy was first. His hands shook as I knelt before him, his mother stood behind him with tears already forming. I placed my palm against his chest, closed my eyes, and waited for that familiar warmth to move from me into him. It came slowly that day—like syrup instead of light, but still, it came.

Each one after took longer than usual. My legs ached more and my breath was labored between patients. The sky above continued to darken, casting a strange color across the ridge. I could feel it: a weight in the air, like the day itself was on hold, and all the while, I could sense him there watching, judging, and condemning.

The final patient was a woman who had been losing her sight for years. When it was done, she opened her eyes and gasped at the color of the ocean, of her own dress, and of the sky itself. At first there was silence, but then a wave of applause came in celebration.

My father stepped forward, uninvited. He lifted one hand and began to shout, but that time, his voice abruptly stopped mid-word. He stumbled as his hand flew to his chest.

I dropped the mic.

"Stay back!" he wheezed. "Don't touch me."

Then he collapsed.

People screamed and the cameraman fumbled to shut off the feed. Reese rushed forward, but I got there first.

I knelt beside him. "Martin. Let me help."

"No," he coughed, his face paling. "*Don't… touch me…*"

And then, a presence moved past me. It was Albert.

He was barefoot and calm, his thick hair windblown, and his face unreadable. He knelt beside him and looked into the eyes of the man who had done everything to shame us.

"You don't have to believe in him." Albert said. "But I believe in you *grandfather*."

He reached out and touched Martin's chest with one hand. It lasted only seconds, but when it was over, the color had returned to his face, his breathing had evened and his eyes had opened.

Albert stood, said nothing else, and returned to his seat.

The crowd was silent, and no one moved.

My father didn't speak; he just lay there, breathing deep as if it were the first time he'd had that luxury in a while. I knew then it was most certainly lung cancer. That is what I'd smelled on him before.

He didn't look at me; he stared at the sky, as if something he'd built his whole life on had deceived him.

The most surprising thing of the day was that his body received the light *in a good way*. I'm not sure why I expected another Pepper situation. I suppose all I had to go on was what I knew of him or what I projected onto him. I'd only seen anger, spite, and everything opposite of love.

I have to admit, as I write this, it still makes me smile, and it is still quite exciting. It means, he already had the light living within him.

***

Reese stood quietly at the edge of the bluff long after the others had gone.

The wind whipped around his collar. He was supposed to be taking statements and reviewing footage, but instead, he was thinking of Rory.

At sixteen years old, he was still afraid of thunder and still asking if Mom was coming home.

Rory cried the first time Reese shaved his

face and laughed the second, and since then it had become their Sunday ritual: after cartoons, before pancakes. Reese still used the cheap yellow razor because Rory said the electric one tickled too much.

Reese wasn't angry, not really; he was torn.

He imagined Rory at home, looking up at the same sky, probably through his bedroom window, wondering where his brother had gone and waiting on him. Maybe he knew, because as strange as it was, he had always been gifted with seeing and knowing things unseen or unknown by *"regular"* folks. And if he did, maybe he was questioning why the man he trusted most hadn't told him that there were certain people with magic inside of them or that hearts could stop and start again with a single touch.

And Reese, who had held Rory through seizures, silent stares, and nights of soft prayers, couldn't help but ask the question that had been quietly tearing him apart.

If he could be healed, **should he be?**

33.

After that day, my father was a believer and a consistent presence in our lives. A good one.

It didn't happen gradually; it happened all at once. Something inside him broke open during that fall, and whatever light entered through that fracture stayed there, and mixed with his own. Overnight, he became everything I had ever needed in a father.

He didn't apologize for the past, not directly, but in every way that mattered, he showed up for all of us.

He was an affectionate grandfather and Himala adored him. She would sit at his feet while he told her stories from the Old Testament, stopping every so often to make sure she was following along. She rarely answered, but she would stare up at him mesmerized and usually rest her head against his knee. His voice soothed her, and her presence softened his soul.

Thomas asked him hard questions about God, death, and war. Albert wanted to talk about theology and physics and where they intersected, and my father found a way to be present for all of it.

Also, after that day, we had no choice but to expand the way we handled healing. The gatherings doubled in size and frequency and we began to hold the sessions twice a week. We'd cleared a new section of the bluff, built wooden benches, and laid gravel paths. We tried to balance logistics, commitment, and personal boundaries, and it seemed to work. It became a well-oiled machine of pure love, but it took its toll on me.

I was thinning out again and I was weak and sick most of the time. My joints ached with a familiar stiffness, and my reflection seemed older with every sunrise. I could feel what the gift was doing to me deep inside.

But oddly enough, the crowds no longer lingered at the bottom of the ridge and we weren't being stalked or harassed. There were no more picket lines, no more shouted scripture, and people respected our space. They came with reverence, not entitlement.

On occasion, someone would arrive with an infant who otherwise wouldn't survive the night, and my father was always the one to welcome them. He didn't want to be the reason someone missed the opportunity, so, much of the time he stayed at Stans place. Spending most of his night hours scanning for emergency arrivals.

He'd meet them quietly at the base of the stairs, no matter what time of day or night it was. He'd wrap them in one of our handmade quilts and carry them up the hill. He brought them to me with such softness, I barely recognized the man I once feared.

I didn't ask questions and never protested. I simply did what was needed, but it was obvious I was running low. I started to drift in and out of exhaustion between sessions. I barely ate and often woke in the middle of the night drenched in sweat from fever.

I have to say that sometimes even the most educated people have trouble seeing the forest through the trees. I'm talking about me — I was the blind one.

I knew the signs. I knew it was the beginning of the end. Until, out of the blue, the signs seemed to give me a reprieve.

It started subtly with a few better days in a row. The heaviness in my body seemed to lift and my heart was not racing every time I climbed the steps. I chalked it up to adrenaline or possibly some final burst of strength before the long goodbye, but it continued. I started to feel *better*, not worse. I felt stronger and more myself and it didn't make sense. Until the evening that Leigh shed some light on the matter.

We were folding laundry, the children were already in bed, and she was unusually quiet.

"I need to tell you something," she said, carefully folding a pair of Albert's socks.

I looked at her, waiting.

"It's Albert. He's been coming to you at night after you fall asleep."

It took me a minute for her words to register.

"What do you mean?" I asked.

"He places his hands on you. Over your heart or your head for a few minutes."

I stopped folding.

"He doesn't wake you, and I pretend that I'm sleeping," she continued. "He doesn't want you to know. He gives you a little of himself, just enough to keep you going."

I had to sit down.

"How long?"

"Months," she said. "Since before your father's fall."

I couldn't speak.

My boy was healing me.

He wasn't saving the world; he was saving me, and it had never once entered my mind. But something else was bothering me that I hadn't mentioned.

My father wasn't getting younger. His physical appearance remained the same; he was just healthier.

Was it possible that Albert could control the amount of light used, or did he have some internal ability to know how much was needed for healing and what was overkill?

I'm pretty sure Leigh validated my suspicions with that conversation. But honestly, I was more intrigued than I was stunned.

34.

For a while, it was happiness.

Not the loud sort you post about or try to hold onto too tightly. It was the soft daily kind. The kind you recognize after it's gone.

We had reached a point in our lives that we were content with two healing sessions a week and quiet days in between. I woke up with strength in my body again, not because the gift had stopped taking from me — but because Albert was quietly giving back, and I let him.

The garden flourished and the hens began laying again after a long lull. Himala learned the names of the herbs we grew by scent alone, and Thomas and Albert argued over compost strategy like old men over a game of checkers.

And then something new began.

Thomas, at six years old, started to show the first signs. It was subtle at first. A bird with a broken wing that he refused to leave behind.

He'd sat with the little guy for nearly an hour, petting and calming him. I'd chalked it up to innocence and stubborn compassion, but the next morning, that bird was flying around the porch.

Then came the stray dog with the mangled paw, the lizard missing its tail, a young deer with an infected wound... and frogs. I've never seen so many frogs!

One by one, Thomas sat quietly, placed his hand near the injured spot and waited. Not with performance or knowledge, but instinct.

I got to see firsthand how our land had become a menagerie. Once healed, the animals stayed. They just don't leave, and croaking became a very loud part of our evening serenade.

Albert watched with a mixture of pride and what I can only assume was worry.

"They're not supposed to come into it this young," he said to me one night. "Are they?"

"I wasn't ready when it happened to me," I admitted. "And neither were you, and Albert — you were three."

Thomas, unlike either of us, was joyful about it. No fear and no weight. It was just something he *could* do, like skipping stones or solving puzzles. The gift was evolving, or perhaps we were.

The people who came to the ridge had grown gentler too. There was no longer the desperation in their eyes or the entitlement. It had become sacred again.

And then, one Thursday morning, it all changed.

Martin was doing his normal daily scan of the area below with his binoculars when he saw a white car with a government emblem pull up to the bottom of the ridge.

We didn't think much of it at first; people arrived unannounced all the time. But the woman who stepped out had a badge, a clipboard, and the solid posture of someone who had done this many times before.

She climbed the steps and introduced herself as a caseworker from Child Protective Services. Officer Reese was with her.

"We've had an anonymous tip," she said,

flipping through her folder. "Concerns about the welfare of the children on this property. Specifically, education and medical care."

My mouth dried out. Albert stood nearby, frozen, and Leigh's face did not hide her shock.

"I'd like to ask a few questions," the woman continued, "and take a look around, if that's alright."

Leigh stepped forward, and like the day in my office years before, I saw a glimpse of the tornado in her mannerisms. She immediately turned into a mama bear.

"May I ask what this is about, exactly?"

"There's no record of school enrollment for the children, no immunization records or pediatric appointments, and no formal documentation since the birth of..." She paused to look at her paperwork, then looked over her glasses and said, "Albert."

"He's homeschooled," Leigh said. "And we live off-grid."

"Yes," the woman replied. "That's part of the concern."

She didn't come across as cruel, just clinical.

I touched Leigh on the shoulder and squeezed; I needed her to calm down.

We all walked into the house, where the woman asked to speak with Albert alone, and then Thomas. She jotted notes and occasionally raised a brow, but she was pretty straightforward.

When it came to Himala, it was a whole different attitude entirely. She seemed uncomfortable with our daughter and avoided eye contact when she spoke of her.

Two hours later, she closed her folder and sighed.

"You seem like a loving, capable family, but the lack of paperwork, vaccinations, and traditional oversight puts you in a vulnerable position. There's going to be a follow-up."

"What does that mean?" I asked.

"It means you'll be under review. If you don't bring your children into compliance with state requirements, there could be consequences. I will assign a special needs professional to do a well-check on Himala."

After handing us her card, she left. Officer

Reese lingered for a moment, as if he was going to say something, but he didn't. He turned away and followed her down the steps, latching the gate behind them.

Leigh reached for my hand, and I could feel the tremble in hers.

That night, when the house was quiet, the two of us sat on the porch.

"We're not putting them in school," Leigh said angrily. "And I'm not letting them inject anything into Albert."

"I know," I replied.

"So, what now?"

I looked up at the stars.

It had always been coming, in one form or another. The day when our life would no longer fit inside the world's rules. At that point we had to decide what to do about it, and it was terrifying.

All good things must come to an end.

35.

The second visit came without warning.

That time, it wasn't about education or immunization. The woman from CPS was different than the first, and she was focused entirely on Himala.

She arrived mid-morning, just after breakfast, which would have been fine any other day of the year, but not that one.

Leigh answered the door with Himala in her arms; she was wrapped in a quilt, her cheeks were unusually pink, and her breathing was shallow.

"She has a fever," Leigh explained nervously. "We were about to start a cool compress and check her again in an hour."

The woman didn't look convinced as she peered over her glasses. She'd introduced herself without warmth, and honestly, to this day, I could not tell you her name; neither of us heard it over our panic.

"We received a report of medical neglect. I need to see the child."

Leigh didn't argue, but I could see the fear in her eyes. Still, she stepped aside.

The woman's eyes scanned Himala, then widened slightly. She stepped closer, inspecting her lips, her fingers, and her breathing. She asked a few routine questions, which Leigh answered calmly, but then her radio buzzed, and she stepped outside and spoke quickly into the receiver.

Within twenty minutes, paramedics and Reese were climbing the ridge.

"I didn't call them." I yelled out in fear and frustration. "We're handling it."

"You no longer have the authority to make that decision," the woman said coldly.

They took our child from Leigh's arms.

Stunned and panicked, Himala cried out. A low, heartbreaking shriek.

I tried to follow, but they blocked me. They told us to wait and that the hospital would contact us after intake. That "any interference may jeopardize your rights."

I stood on the gravel, fists clenched, and watched as the ambulance took my daughter away and disappeared around the bend of the road. They didn't even let us ride with her.

That night, the wind howled across the cliffs, and none of us slept.

Albert sat at the kitchen table, staring at the same page in a book for hours, unmoving. Thomas cried himself to sleep in Leigh's lap as I walked the perimeter of the ridge three times, not knowing what else to do with the rage inside of me.

The next morning brought no news — only a formal letter delivered by courier:

Temporary Protective Custody Enacted.
Diagnosis: Congenital Heart Defect.
Condition: Angina due to compromised blood flow.
Visitation: Postponed until stabilization and clearance by attending physicians. Supervised visitation only, with Child Protective Services present.

No timeline and no room for argument.

They had our daughter, and they wouldn't even let us *see* her. The pain settled in like fog and clung to everything. Our meals grew quieter and our mornings slower. The house that had once been filled with song and laughter echoed with absence.

Grandpa Martin was shattered and spent each evening in the circle where we normally held healings, kneeling with his Bible, holding candlelight prayer vigils under the fading sun.

He wept openly. She had become his favorite, with her innocence and complete adoration for him.

By the third day, others from town began to join him — those we'd helped and those who believed in us. A quiet vigil grew into something larger, but no one could touch the ache in his voice when he prayed aloud for her safe return.

"My granddaughter," he whispered each night. "Lord, my lamb with the purest heart. Watch over her, forgive this world its cruelty, and bring her home."

Leigh moved through the house like a ghost. She still made meals and she still tucked Thomas in at night, but she did not sing, and

Albert didn't even care to pick up a book. Part of our family had been taken; they were wounded without her.

I, too, was something less than functional.

Each day without Himala felt lonely. Each breath I took while she was locked away felt labored. We were a family bound in light, and without her, we were dimmer, unstable, and broken.

Court was scheduled.

But there was no Himala.

We had to show up, argue, and beg for the right to see our own child. The child who had *thrived* under our care, the child who had never known fear until they took her. Yet, all we could do was wait.

And the worst of it was that it was our fault. An unbelievable truth was that in all of our healing, none of us ever recognized or considered she would have a heart problem, and that fact alone worked against us. We needed to see her to heal what was inside of her before it was too late. Before we lost her from this world, and I don't mean to a foster family or facility.

36.

The courthouse was beige and impersonal, of course it was — with fluorescent lighting, outdated carpet, and the faint smell of burnt coffee drifting in from a nearby break room.

We sat in the family waiting area for nearly forty minutes before they called our case. Leigh didn't speak; she stared at her hands, folded neatly in her lap. Albert sat beside me in a chair that was too small. His brow was furrowed so tightly that it looked painful, and he was chewing on the inside of his cheek. Thomas had been left with a neighbor near the ridge. He didn't need any more trauma.

When our names were called, we walked into a room that felt like a theater. A judge sat behind the bench with the weariness of someone who'd heard it all before. A CPS lawyer stood with a file already open, and across the room sat two strangers: a pediatric specialist from the hospital and a court-appointed guardian ad litem, who had visited Himala twice.

We were sworn in.

The CPS representative began.

"The child in question, Himala Harper, was removed from the home due to immediate medical concerns. At the time of her removal, she was suffering with a high fever, shallow breathing, and visible signs of distress. There was no record of regular checkups, no immunization history, and no hospital or pediatric documentation in her file. Her condition — diagnosed as congenital angina — was severe and previously undetected."

Those words hit and hurt; I had a lump in my throat and fought back tears.

"She is now stabilized, but due to the gravity of the medical oversight and the family's prior refusal to engage with standard healthcare routines, such as vaccinations, we recommend continued protective custody until full compliance can be verified and the court is confident of the child's welfare."

Leigh took the stand next. She was clear,

composed, and calm. She explained our lifestyle, our beliefs, and our history of healing without embellishment or arrogance. She simply told the truth.

The judge asked her if she had any formal medical training. She said no. Then he asked if she understood how dangerous it could be to miss a condition like Himala's. She shifted nervously in her seat.

"Yes, your Honor. I understand that now."

When it was my turn, I was honest about everything as well.

I told him I'd made mistakes in the past. That I had been given something I didn't completely understand, something I'd tried to use only for good, and that my children were never neglected, never unloved, and never unsafe.

"I would die for her," I said.

The judge didn't look up when I said it.

He did look over his glasses at each of us when we spoke of the gift of healing, but mostly he kept his head down scribbling notes. We all saw what he was really thinking.

His facial expressions silently questioned our sanity, and he didn't even try to hide it.

Albert spoke last. No one asked him to, but he'd asked for permission. The courtroom held its breath as he walked to the stand.

"I'm twelve," he said. "And I know what you're thinking. That I'm too young to understand responsibility, but I helped raise my sister. I taught her to play piano. I helped her learn words, identify birds, and taste the difference between spearmint and peppermint in the garden. She's not just a case; she's my sister, and you're hurting her by keeping her from us even if you think you're helping—can't you see that? She must be scared; she's never been away from us."

He wiped his eyes with the sleeve of his shirt.

After a long pause in activity, the judge thanked Albert and told us that a supervised visit would be scheduled the following week, but only if her doctors deemed her stable enough to interact with family.

And that was it.

We weren't allowed to see her that day. We weren't told if she was asking for us. We were simply handed another paper and asked to leave.

Outside the courthouse, Martin was waiting.

He pulled me into a hug so tight I couldn't breathe. Leigh cried into his chest, and he held her.

That night, he lit three small torches in the circle outside and prayed aloud again. Repeating his plea over and over.

"Lord, don't let her forget our voices," he said. "Don't let her spirit go dim in a place that doesn't know how to hold her."

Albert stood nearby, not speaking, but behind his silence, I could sense a storm beginning to gather in him.

37.

The hospital smelled like bleach and rubbing alcohol and it was nauseating.

They'd moved her to a children's wing on the fourth floor; behind a glass security door we had to be buzzed through twice. Posters of smiling animals lined the hallway walls, but they didn't fool anyone; even the cartoons looked tired and misleading.

We were only allowed two visitors, no negotiation.

Leigh and Albert went while I stayed in the hallway pacing, trying not to lose my mind. A caseworker shadowed them into the room, and a nurse stood nearby with a tablet in her hand, logging her vitals.

I watched through the small rectangular window in the door. Himala was propped up in a metal-framed bed, her arms limp at her sides, her eyes red from crying. Tubes trailed out from under her blankets. Her cheeks were pale, and her lips were dry.

When she saw Leigh, she lit up. She reached out and her little stocky fingers shook.

Leigh rushed to her side and scooped her into her arms, careful of the wires and IVs, pressing her lips to her forehead. Himala clung to her like she might never let go.

She sobbed, not from pain, but from recognition, from reunion and confusion—she didn't understand any of it.

Leigh rocked her gently as Albert stood at the foot of the bed, his hands at his sides, his face unreadable.

The doctor stepped in quickly, frowning. "We need to calm her down; this level of distress isn't good for her heart. We may need to sedate her."

"No," Leigh replied sharply. "Please, please, just a few more minutes; she needs this."

But the nurse was already prepping a syringe.

"Let us step out," the caseworker said, motioning to Albert and Leigh.

Himala screamed as they tried to lower her back into the bed.

"Ma-ma," she wailed. "Ma—don't go—Ma!"

Leigh broke. I saw the excruciating heartbreak in her eyes.

Still, Albert didn't move.

Instead, as the nurse turned to check a chart and the doctor reached for the IV line, he stepped forward and placed one hand gently over Himala's heart. Not for long, just a few meaningful seconds.

Her crying softened, and her breathing slowed.

She looked up at him, her expression less panicked, and whispered something that I couldn't hear.

Then the door opened, and a nurse ushered them out.

Leigh was sobbing. Albert looked calm, but his face was flushed, his eyes glassy.

As they crossed the threshold into the hallway, the CPS worker turned.

"What did he do?"

But it was too late, and we were already

walking.

She had no proof. Just one child a little more at peace, and that's all it ever needed to be.

He didn't fix her; she wasn't broken, and he didn't try to erase her condition. He knew better.

Albert had done exactly what we came to do and gave her enough to rest. Enough to heal at her pace, in her own way. We loved Himala as she was, and he, more than any of us, knew how to give her only what she needed — no more, no less.

A gift we still didn't understand, living inside the heart of a twelve-year-old boy.

38.

They discharged her two days later. Not home and not to us, but to a state-run facility for children with special needs. They called it "Temporary housing," which was supposed to be a safe, supportive environment while the court made its final decision.

No one asked us what we thought.

The CPS worker barely made eye contact when she showed up to inform us.

"She's stable. More than stable, actually," she said. "The improvement was unexpected. She's eating and responsive, and her heart rhythm has regulated. The doctors are optimistic and surprised — to say the least. But protocol is protocol."

We asked if we could come get her, and she told us no.

"She's being moved to Ridgewood Therapeutic Home," she added. "Supervised visitation is three hours weekly and will start next Monday."

We left, and Leigh didn't speak for hours.

She sat outside Stan's house, wrapped in one of Himala's blankets, rocking back and forth in the wicker chair. Her eyes were open, but she wasn't really there.

I chopped wood for no other reason than to try and work off the feeling of helplessness. By the time the sun set, I had a mountain of logs and a blistered palm.

Albert disappeared out of sight for most of the day, and when he returned, his cheeks were flushed and his hands were muddy. He wouldn't say where he'd been.

Thomas was everywhere we were. His twin was gone, and for him, it left him feeling as though half of himself was missing. He was dazed and exceptionally quiet.

We were all coming apart in our own ways.

***

Martin came by that night with stew and support. He stayed long after sundown, sitting in the circle beside the cold firepit, his hat in his lap. I joined him.

"I don't understand," he said quietly. "I prayed, I fasted, and I begged, and she got better. She *got better*, and still, they took her away?"

I didn't answer; I couldn't. There was no comfort I could give and no logic to explain.

"They want to believe they're saving her," I finally said. "That's the part that stings."

Leigh came outside just after midnight; her eyes were red but dry.

"I want to bring her home," she said. "Even if it means we disappear."

Martin looked at me with Thomas half asleep in his lap, and so did Albert, who had stepped out silently from behind her — and in that moment, I knew it; we all did.

This wasn't about healing anymore. It was about whether we could survive loving someone so much the world called it a threat.

39.

Ridgewood was two towns over. A brick building with a high, locked fence and a security gate out front. The type of place that was trying too hard not to look like what it was. The state called it care; we called it exile.

The lawn was clean but sparse, the trees were trimmed too precisely, and the whole place felt like it had been sanitized of joy. It reeked of an asylum from a bygone era, and it made me queasy.

We were only allowed inside for up to an hour each, one at a time.

Leigh went first. I waited with Albert and Thomas in the gray hallway, counting the minutes by watching the second hand on a clock that ticked too loudly. When she came back out, she looked positively ill.

"She's slipping," she said. "Her body's okay, but she won't speak. She wouldn't even look me in the eyes."

Albert went in next. He didn't say anything when he came out, and on our way home, he sat in the back of the car and stared out the window with his hands folded tightly in his lap. We knew we couldn't wait much longer.

Thomas was the only one that got a response from her; she looked at him with complete recognition, but it was as if she were sedated. She bowed her head, teared up, and said,

"Princetie. You."

That night, after Thomas was in bed, we sat around the table. It was Leigh, Albert, Martin, and I, and no one needed to ask what we were discussing. The decision was already made. We were going to bring her home one way or another.

"She can't survive there," Leigh said. "Not really. Even if they keep her body healthy, they're killing her spirit."

"She gets her strength from us," Albert added, and we do from her. Thomas is barely speaking now. He hasn't smiled since she left."

It was true. Our home felt hollow without

her, and Thomas had become a shell. His laughter was gone; his appetite nil. He slept in her bed, curled up on her pillow like a child half his age.

"They won't let us walk out with her," I said. "Not legally."

"Then we stop waiting for permission," Martin said.

We discussed every option, to include roads, airstrips, and friends of friends, but in the end, we all agreed that the best answer was a boat. Something modest and capable of long travel and possibly a new life in another country. After the decision was made, it didn't take long.

We found a retired fishing vessel down the coast still in decent shape; we paid cash, no paperwork. We slowly stocked it with supplies, fuel, and enough gear to disappear. We bought in bits and pieces, over weeks, through different vendors in different towns.

I spent every second poring over old manuals, books, and media to learn what I needed to know to captain such a vessel. I learned the intricate details of the navigation system, and I honed my mechanical skills to the point that if I had to, I could rebuild the engine from the ground up. I was beyond prepared.

Albert helped organize the route, and Martin kept lookout and covered our stories.

Leigh gathered medicines, packed clothing, and salt-cured or smoked fish and meat. She wrote down recipes and gospel hymns she'd grown to love, especially the ones Martin sang to Himala.

Every night we returned to the table and rechecked the plan and lists, and every day that passed without our daughter, we felt her slipping further away.

The staff at Ridgewood reported that she was "uncooperative." That she stared at walls and refused to eat unless someone sang to her. They asked if we'd had her psychologically assessed. They began talking in terms like "disassociation" and "*long-term dependency*," as if her joy, speech, and interaction had always been a fluke.

They didn't understand her; they couldn't possibly understand unless they had known her before.

Thomas was getting worse.

He stopped saving animals in need, he wouldn't go near the garden and he'd begun wetting the bed again, though he tried to hide it. He carried around one of Himala's old hair bows in his pocket like it was the last part of her he could still hold onto.

So, we pushed forward. We worked faster and harder, and by week's end, everything was ready.

The final plans were made just before dawn as Martin stood with me by the old wooden fence, looking out at the water.

"So, the next visit, you'll take her, but I have to ask, son. Exactly how do you intend to do that?"

He shifted around, put one boot up on the fence, and leaned against it. He seemed to be ready for whatever I was about to confess, and I'm sure my words didn't comfort him the way he needed. He was concerned; we'd never discussed that part of the plan.

I cleared my throat and answered,

"The less you know, the better off you'll be. I don't need you culpable. The only way to keep you safe is for you to be ignorant concerning certain details. In case anything goes wrong, I might need you to take care of my family."

"I'll stay," he said simply, ignoring what I'd told him. "I'll take the houses and the land and turn this place into what it always should've been, a place for the ones who don't fit anywhere else."

"You'll be watched," I said.

"I'm a preacher," he replied. "They've been watching me half of my life."

I grinned, because I had to agree with his last statement.

"You're sure?"

"She's my granddaughter," he said. "You're my son, and this place changed me. I won't let it die empty."

We shook hands and let it go.

***

Late that night we got a phone call from a woman whose voice I didn't recognize. She said she didn't want to have the conversation over the phone and asked to meet us at dawn. She needed to tell us something important that would help. I agreed, hung up, and went next door to tell my father.

He put his hand on my shoulder, squeezed it, and said what anyone who knew him would expect him to say.

"Son, the Lord works in mysterious ways, and I hope whatever he's got up his sleeve will let our girl come back to her family where she belongs."

Then he followed that with,

"And they can all go to Hades."

He smiled and made another comment about how un-Christian that must sound, quickly apologized to the Lord, looking toward the heavens, and then wrapped me in a long-overdue hug. The kind of hug that I'd waited for my whole life; the kind that *I* pulled away from *first*.

If more people only understood the power of having someone hold on *longer* than you do in a hug.

It is magic: Forgiving, validating, pure love.
I hope whoever reads these words
remembers those last ones. They are so
important.

40.

We met her at first light, just past the outer trail, where the wild ferns swallow the path in early spring.

She wore hospital scrubs under a heavy coat, her hair tied back in a knot, her eyes darting behind us every few seconds. She wasn't what I expected. She was young, maybe in her early thirties, with worry lines already grooved into her brow and kindness she couldn't hide even if she tried.

"My name is Rachel; my son's name is Nick. Two years ago, you healed his congenital scoliosis, and he walks now."

I remembered him. A quiet boy who'd barely spoken. I recalled vividly the way she cried when he took his first pain-free steps outside the garden. The love and the energy from that day enveloped me as she spoke.

"I owe you everything," she said. "I've never

forgotten. So, when I saw your daughter's name assigned to me, I knew it wasn't a coincidence, and I knew I had to help. It's the least I can do."

Leigh stood solid and aching beside me, stiff as stone, her arms crossed against the wind.

"She's not doing well," Rachel continued. "They say she's stable, but I see it. She's sad and sedated, and she won't talk. She doesn't even cry; she just lies there with her eyes open."

"She's dying inside," Leigh said, emotion making her voice quiver.

Rachel nodded in agreement.

"I want to help," she said. "But it has to be exact. There's one night this week, on Thursday, that I'll be on overnight duty and in charge of bed checks. After that, they assume the children are asleep. I can take her from the west wing, through the laundry corridor, and out the back delivery ramp."

"Are there cameras?" Albert asked.

"There are," she said. "But I've already mapped the gaps, and I know the shift patterns. Once I bring her, you'll have about eight hours before anyone notices."

She pulled out folded papers from her pocket and handed them to me. A hand-drawn layout of the facility, areas to avoid, and staff rotations. It was too dark to make out what the other pages were, but she explained.

"Because we are a state institution, we get all of the patient's records; those are certified copies of birth certificates. I think your sons was sent by accident because they're twins with the same birthday. I knew you would want them."

"You'll need to be waiting two blocks east, behind the maintenance shed. If you're late, I can't stall. If she's not gone by 11:30, the door locks from the inside, and I can't risk them catching me with her."

We thanked her, all at once. For a few seconds it was a group family whisper of our gratitude. She was a manifestation in real time of the emotion and intention we had put out into the universe with our type of work. Every detail was already cemented into our minds, and with tears in her eyes, Leigh asked,

"Why are you doing this? You could lose everything."

Rachel's voice softened.

"Because I *have* everything because of you. I couldn't live with myself if I didn't help bring her back where she belongs."

Before she left, she paused and turned to Albert.

"You're the boy with the hands," she said. "Aren't you?"

He met her eyes but said nothing.

She smiled, lightly touched his shoulder, and then walked the path around the ridge, vanishing from sight.

That night, we finalized everything. The new plan was a heck of a lot better than the old one. But still, no one slept.

The boys were bathed and laid on the couch, whispering to one another.

Martin prepared the fuel stores and locked the journals in a trunk in the cabin's foundation.

"This is the last time we look back, and we have to move fast," he said, setting the latch.

By morning, the wind had shifted. It carried the salty scent of the ocean stronger than ever, and we were all on edge.

Three more days, and then we'd have her back. Those were the longest three days of our lives.

41.

We harvested everything we could. The garden, barely clinging to life after the last frost, gave up its roots reluctantly. Carrots, herbs, onions, and a few hard pears from the tree behind the shed. Leigh worked in silence, sleeves rolled high, her hands dark with soil. Albert trailed her with a basket, and Thomas followed behind him with a pencil and paper, taking inventory.

"We'll have to eat the pears early," he said. "They'll rot first."

I watched him adjust the weight in the backpack he'd prepared, one object at a time — shifting jars and folding blankets, setting aside anything sentimental that wouldn't serve a purpose. He had the sort of focus I envied. No panic, only precision.

"We aren't running," he said to Thomas. "We're relocating; there's a difference."

Leigh looked up at me when he said it, and

for a second, I thought she might cry, but she didn't. She simply pulled up the last of the radishes, stood, and placed them in the basket.

Martin spent the day reinforcing the dock ramp with plywood and rolled the last fuel drums onto the boat. He pulled a handkerchief from his breast pocket and wiped his brow.

"When you see the stars change," he said, "consult your map. There's no other way to explain that. You'll just know."

I nodded my understanding, and it seems I'd been doing that a lot lately. My mind was everywhere, overanalyzing and rehashing the plan repeatedly.

Inside, the house looked like it had been stripped for auction. Half the kitchenware was packed in sealed bins and already down on the boat, and the walls were bare. The boys' books were down to ten each, and Leigh had rolled their clothes into tight bundles marked by ribbon.

At some point, she'd cut her hair and I watched her braid the shortened strands and tuck them beneath a cap. She caught me staring and said, "What?"

I shook my head, kissed her on the forehead and told her how much the short hair suited her.

We knew we weren't simply leaving a place; we were leaving names and the thick paper walls of legality. We would be listed as kidnappers for taking our own daughter, and it scared me to think about. From the day we left until the end of time, we would be fugitives. I had to keep telling myself we weren't *taking* Himala; we were *bringing her home*.

Albert carved small totem animals from dry wood and painted their eyes with soot. He lined them in a row beside his bed and whispered their names before falling asleep. He'd tied one of the sage charms to the boat rail the day before and told Thomas not to touch it until we'd cleared the open sea.

"It won't work until she's back with us," he said. "The magic's incomplete."

I have no idea where that idea came from. I suspected it was from a book, but not from any I'd read. Either way, I didn't interfere in his self-soothing process.

That night, Thomas sat up beside me while I went over the route again. His voice was soft and curious, but he wasn't a baby anymore.

"Will it be warm there?"

"Most of the year."

"Will they have figs?"

"Probably."

"Good," he said. "I think she'll like figs."

He stopped squirming and looked down at the floor.

"I had another dream last night," he said. "She wasn't scared this time; she was waiting."

"Where?"

He looked up. "Near the boat, she was sitting like she knew."

I didn't say anything. I just pulled him closer and let him rest against me while the wind moved around the corners of the house.

Leigh laid out the final supplies: water canisters, vitamins, rolled oats, a tin of powdered milk, and the last two jars of blackberry preserves from last summer. We had a generator on the boat, a full kitchen, and all of the staples we could possibly need.

I added the documents Rachel had given us, along with a burner phone, charged and wrapped in cloth.

I remember thinking how odd it felt to hold the phone when a cell phone used to be an extension of my hand. I hadn't considered my cellphone in years; I didn't need to. We had a landline in both homes for appointments and emergencies, and that served us well enough. We really were living in our own world; we didn't fit in.

We packed silently, each in our own mind about the *how or if* we would succeed, but definitely not about the *why*. When it was done, the remaining bags lined the wall and the air in my lungs had a new weight to it. Heavier than anxiety and sharper than fear.

I looked at the clock…thirty-two hours to go.

Martin came in from the cold, set a match to the hearth, and said,

"We can't rest now; we need to get these provisions loaded tonight under the cover of darkness. Tomorrow night, it's showtime."

Leigh took one last look at the baby blanket

folded on top of Himala's pack.

"We're not running," she said, repeating Thomas's words. "We're relocating as a complete family."

***

Reese had been a welcome guest among us for months and never missed a healing session. He was there when Himala was taken by ambulance, and I'm sure that wasn't a coincidence. I believe he wanted things to go smoothly. He cared for us, with a special affection for our daughter, but as an officer, he didn't miss a thing. Behaviors that others wouldn't even consider, he noticed immediately.

He was there when Martin made cash withdrawals at the bank or ran to town to fill up more drums with fuel. Something we didn't know until later.

I suppose he was in a horrible position; I see that now.

He was fighting an inner war between his heart and his mind, and it was tearing him up.

It's no wonder that all he saw in the end was that *the man and the boy, who possessed the gifts, were preparing to leave*. It all came down to his brother Rory.

Each evening, Martin watched curiously through binoculars as Reese paced by his pickup for hours at the bottom of the bluff.

And each and every one of those nights, Reese would pull his coat tighter, get into his truck, and turn back toward town.

42.

The final day passed like a slow-motion nightmare. There wasn't enough oxygen; I swear, no other description will fit that feeling.

We went through the motions as if nothing had changed, as if the air wasn't tighter and time wasn't ticking faster. The boys fed the animals, Leigh swept the porch and Martin repaired a section of the fence that had needed mending for five years. No one mentioned what was coming. That was the rule for the day; we didn't say it aloud.

We had to be careful. Anyone driving by, any curious ranger, any volunteer from the nearby wildlife reserve, or even a nosey neighbor might notice something if we broke routine. So, we moved like shadows within our own lives.

Albert spent most of the morning at the waterline, checking the dock ropes, adjusting knots, and testing the crank on the small inflatable raft we'd lashed to the side of the fishing boat. The tide was lower than it should be, and he was obsessively preparing.

Thomas stayed close to Leigh, helping her dry dishes and package the last of the food. She didn't speak much, but she touched his hair when he passed and held her hand on his shoulder a moment too long every time he came near. They had their own language and nothing needed to be verbalized.

Martin sharpened his hunting knife. It wasn't for defense; it seemed to be a nervous or habitual tic.

I stayed inside most of the day, pacing from the front door to the back window. I checked and rechecked the bag of documents and recounted the money Martin withdrew for us.

The sun moved too fast. My thoughts kept skipping ahead. What if she cried when she saw us? What if she didn't want to go? What if she didn't know who we were anymore?

By late afternoon, a truck rolled slowly up the gravel road below, and my anxiety kicked in. Not only because we hadn't gotten Himala yet, but because there are certain people you never expect to see again, especially not on the eve of an illegal escape.

Our nerves settled some when we saw that it was Donna's sister, Marianne. We hadn't seen her since the funeral. She parked on the road and made her way up the steps, carrying something wrapped in a dishtowel. When she made it through the gate, she looked exhausted. Her face was thinner than I remembered, but she smiled when she saw Leigh and the boys.

"I was passing through," she said. "Thought I'd drop this off. It's apricot. Donna used to say it tasted like sunshine."

If she knew anything, she kept it to herself, but she couldn't keep her eyes from roaming. She seemed to notice things were askew, and she stared into the house through our kitchen window a moment too long.

We invited her to stay for a cup of coffee, which was polite and *normal* behavior.

Thomas sat stiffly beside me, as if unsure how to act *normal* now that normal had become a costume.

"The place hasn't changed," Marianne said, still looking around. She'd obviously figured it out but continued to make small talk. "It still smells like rosemary and old wood. I used to love coming up here."

Albert brought her a fork; she took one polite bite and set the plate down. We all exchanged glances, expecting her to force one of us to lie.

"I won't stay long; I just wanted to see you."

We waited.

She looked at Leigh. "I... I'm not sure how to put this."

Leigh understood before we did. She reached for her hand and told her,

"You're amongst family; speak plainly, we are here to help."

Her next words didn't make sense to me yet; I wasn't in the healing persona. I guess I was the slowest one in our bunch that day. I was struck dumb.

"I didn't understand at first," she said. "None of us did, but knowing you all and then seeing the miracles..." She trailed off. "It's real, isn't it?"

Okay, my mind finally caught up.

She stood and glanced toward the edge of the bluff.

"Donna loved it here."

She didn't have to say more; Albert closed the distance between them with a few strides, reached for her hands, and asked,

"What is it?

Marianne's eyes filled with tears, ready to spill over. She cleared her throat and answered,

"I have colorectal cancer, and I am too young to die. I don't want to die; I'm not ready."

Albert smiled and told her,

"That's my specialty."

He guided her to stand. I immediately walked over and stood behind her as my son moved and stood firmly in position at her side. He placed one hand gently across her lower torso and one in the same spot on her back. A few minutes went by with her eyes closed, and when it was over, she opened them and grinned.

That feeling of light moving through you, no matter how short or long, always brings a smile.

She hugged each of us, to include Martin, who grumbled but didn't pull away. Then she walked back to her truck, the dishtowel still in her hand, and drove off without another word.

We didn't speak for a while after she left. We sat listening to the birds settling in the trees and the wind raking through the dry leaves.

When the sun began to dip, we all changed our clothes to dark layers. Leigh tied her short hair beneath a beanie, and I carried Himala's pack with the fluffy green blanket she loved so much.

We kissed Martin for luck, or in case things went badly. He didn't say much but pulled me into a long, hard hug, then gripped Leigh's hand as if trying to give her something more than words could express.

"I'll be waiting," he said. "Go get our girl."

We left, and no more words were spoken. Thomas carried a flashlight with a red lens, and Albert wore his carved animal charm around his neck like armor.

We drove through two towns and miles of road in complete silence and turned our headlights off before the last block. We then walked the two miles to the outer street where Rachel had told us to wait. The air was crisp, and the moon was low and veiled behind thin clouds, giving just enough light.

At exactly 11:12 pm, Rachel appeared at the edge of the lot. She moved quickly, with a bundle in her arms. I stepped forward before she spoke and reached for my little girl.

Himala didn't make a sound. She gazed up at me with wide, tired eyes and let me take her into my arms. She was warm, smaller than I remembered, and still smelled faintly sterile, like disinfectant.

Leigh cradled her cheek and whispered her name, and Himala gave a shy smile.

Rachel stepped back.

"No one saw me," she said. "You have until dawn; after that, they'll know."

She handed me one last envelope. "More copies of her medical files. You might need them."

Leigh gripped her hand. "Thank you."

Rachel nodded, eyes glistening. "Take her

somewhere wonderful."

Then she turned and disappeared down the alley without another word.

We didn't run. We just walked quickly, careful not to draw attention since we were so close to the institution. Himala nestled against my chest, her fingers twisting the collar of my coat. Thomas walked behind us, turning every few steps to make sure we weren't followed while Albert led the way.

That car ride back seemed to take forever, but we made it in record time.

The moon broke through the clouds as we reached the top of the trail on the bluff. Martin was there, urging us along. Below us, the boat and the ocean that we were putting our trust into waited.

We had her back, but we only had about four hours before daybreak.

43.

When the Water Glows

They moved in silence down the path, the one worn smooth by time and repetition. Martin walked with them, carrying the last pack slung over his shoulder, boots crunching softly in the sand. The sky was still dark, but the stars had begun to fade, giving way to that gray whisper of coming light. The tide was out. The main vessel sat farther than expected. The fishing boat, their freedom ship, was too heavy to reach by dock and too far to wade.

They had to row.

The smaller skiff was already in the water, bobbing gently, tied off near the driftwood pile where Martin kept it hidden. Thomas climbed in first, taking position at the rear, then Albert followed with Mozart in his lap. Scott stood at the shoreline, Himala resting snugly against his chest like she'd never left.

Leigh stayed behind for one last goodbye. Her arms were draped around Martin with her forehead pressed to his, and her voice was barely audible.

"You saved us," she whispered.

He shook his head. "I helped clear the path; the rest was you."

Then it happened: a man's voice came from nowhere.

"Hey! That's far enough; *stop!*"

Everyone froze.

A flashlight beam cut through the last part of the trail. A figure emerged — gun drawn, voice shouting above the wind.

"Stop right there! Don't move!"

It was Officer Reese, in uniform, shaking and wide-eyed.

"I knew it," he said. "I knew something was going on. The bank withdrawals, the fuel orders… **I can't let you leave!**"

Leigh stepped in front of Scott instinctively, shielding Himala with her arms. Time stood still, and they didn't move a muscle.

Martin raised both hands slowly, stepping

toward Reese like a man calming a wild horse.

"Reese," he said gently, "I've known you since you were a boy. I Watched you chase your brother through the pews at Christ Redeemer, and I still remember your father's prayers."

Reese's hand trembled, but the gun didn't drop.

"It doesn't matter, Pastor. This is kidnapping. I have to call it in."

"Do you? Do you *really need to*, son?" Martin asked gently. "Your brother has Down syndrome, doesn't he?"

Reese looked over at Himala as Scott handed her to Leigh.

"**Look at me**, Reese, **look at** *me*. If they'd taken *him,* if they had taken Rory from you and locked him away without love or family, wouldn't you try everything in your power to bring him home?"

Scott stepped forward, voice steady.

"Leigh, get her to the boat."

Reese turned, panicked.

"Don't move!"

Leigh ran despite his order.

Reese raised the radio to his lips. "Dispatch, I need—"

Martin placed a hand over the mic. His other hand gently pushed the barrel of the gun toward the ground.

"Son," Martin said softly, "don't be the reason this ends in pain."

Reese stood there shaking and breathing hard. Then something in him changed, as if understanding washed over his body. The tension collapsed and then tears came fast and helplessly.

He sank down to the sand cross-legged and buried his face in his hands.

Martin slid down next to him and put his arm around Reese's shoulders, comforting him.

Out on the water, Leigh climbed into the skiff with Himala. Scott followed, pushing off with one final shove before leaping in as the boat began to drift.

That's when the ocean showed its pleasure— in them and in the abundance of good collected in the little rowboat on its surface—the water was alive, and it knew.

The glow started from the depths of darkness, far beneath the surface — slow, soft pulses of bioluminescence, like stars scattered across the sea floor. Then it surged upward. Threads of silver light uncoiled beneath the boat like the limbs of an ancient creature, gently wrapping around the hull. The skiff glided faster, untouched by oars, drawn forward by unseen forces.

The ocean itself was guiding it.

The boys didn't speak. Himala rested her head on Leigh's shoulder, eyes open, unafraid, watching in wonderment.

When they reached the vessel, the lights swelled brighter, reflecting across the deck in streaks of molten silver. Scott hoisted each child aboard, then reached down for Leigh. They moved quickly, in sync, and the boat responded like it had been waiting.

Then the sky joined the incredible scene by opening up.

A single beam of white-gold light poured down from the clouds, not from the moon or even an aircraft, but from somewhere much higher. It caught the vessel in full, bathing it in radiance.

And then, in an instant, they were gone.

No sound, no ripple.

They just vanished.

The water settled, and the light receded. A final shimmer danced across the waves like a million giggles.

Martin rose slowly. Reese wiped his nose on the cuff of his sleeve and stood stunned; tears still streamed down his cheeks.

They said nothing for a while until Martin reached out a hand, and Reese took it.

"I pray that boat was seaworthy." Martin said, smiling.

Reese glanced at the horizon.

"What boat?" He asked, "I didn't see any boat."

They walked back up the path, quietly trying to absorb what they had witnessed. The only sound was a woman's voice coming from his radio.

"Dispatch to Reese — 10-9, over. Reese, 10-9. *Please repeat…* 10-9."

44.

A Letter from Martin Morris,
Dated the night we fled.

You never think you'll be the man who leaves.
Not when you're young and full of fire, not when you
hold your own son in your arms for the first time.
You swear you'll do better than the ones who came
before you. And I meant it. God, I meant it.

I met Irene when Stan was just a little boy – 9 or
10, with those big, watchful eyes. She was raising
him alone, trying to keep it all together with too
much weight on her back and not enough help while
his father was away in the Army. I saw something in
her from the moment we met, not just beauty, though
she had that in spades. She had steel in her spine. She
was a woman who appeared to have not one chink in
her armor. A woman who'd already been through
more than most could handle and kept going anyway.
And then Stan's father got killed in the Gulf War.

I was drawn to her, and we fell fast. I wasn't

looking for anything permanent, not then, but Irene had this way of making everything feel real.

She didn't play games. She told me early on, "I've got a boy. He's my whole world, and if that's a problem, then walk away."

It wasn't a problem. I'd lost my father young, too, and something in me wanted to be what Stan needed, someone stable, someone who stayed — and I did, for a while.

Scott, you came a couple of years later. You were a planned pregnancy, believe it or not. We thought it meant we were doing something right and that we were ready to be a real family.

The day you were born, you barely cried; you looked around the room as if you'd already seen this world before. You wrapped your fingers around mine and held on like I was an anchor.

For a few years, it worked. Not perfectly, but enough.

I worked construction when I could and took side jobs when I couldn't. Irene stayed home with you. Stan called me "Dad" almost from the start, and Scott, you followed your big brother everywhere. But your mom... she began to change.

The cracks showed slowly. At first it was mood

swings. Then long silences, days she wouldn't get out of bed, and nights she paced the hallway until morning. She'd be laughing and kissing my neck one minute, then accusing me of cheating the next, or screaming about everything…or nothing really.

She'd vanish for hours, only to come back dazed, sometimes with bruises she couldn't explain. There were times I thought she might be using something. Other times, I feared it was deeper, something inherited, something you couldn't shake with rest and prayer.

I begged her to get help, and she'd promise to try, but she never did.

I kept working, I kept showing up, but I was tired and scared, and I started failing at everything. I couldn't keep a job, couldn't make the rent, and couldn't hold that house together no matter how badly I wanted to.

Stan, by then, was thirteen. He was too old to be innocent and too young to carry what I placed on his shoulders. He tried to protect his mom, and he tried to protect you, but I watched my stepson become a man before he ever got to be a boy.

You were just a toddler. Quiet, solemn, and so smart it scared me sometimes. You never whined, *never asked for anything. You watched us all crumble from your little corner on the floor.*

And one night... that all changed.

I'd been out looking for work all day and came home to find the power shut off and Irene screaming at shadows in the living room. Stan was holding you in the hallway, soothing you and saying that it would be okay and that he'd take care of you.

That was the moment that convinced me that I was doing more harm than good.

I didn't have the tools or the money, and I didn't have the faith. God help me, I didn't believe I could save any of you. Not your momma, not Stan, not you, and not even me.

So, I left.

Not in a fit of rage, and not with some dramatic goodbye. I packed a bag before dawn and left two envelopes: one with cash and one with a note that said, "I'm sorry. I love you, but I don't know how to help anymore."

It was the most shameful thing I've ever done. Giving up on my wife and children.

I drifted for years after that. Worked odd jobs, slept in shelters, and tried to drink the guilt away. I followed news of Irene when I could and found out she died in 2004 of cancer. I didn't go to the funeral; I didn't think I deserved to.

Eventually, I crawled toward something that looked like redemption. I found my way into a little church shelter, and a preacher there didn't look at me like a lost cause. He believed I still had something worth salvaging. So, I cleaned up, got baptized, and went to seminary in my mid-thirties with a GED and a past full of ghosts.

I didn't do it to become a man of power. I did it to understand forgiveness and to learn how to hold pain without passing it down.

I never stopped thinking about either of you.

I heard Stan became a doctor and got into some sort of trouble, but it forced him back home, where he'd built a quiet life. I always wondered if he ever thought of me, and if so, if he hated me.

And Scott, I dreamed about you. I'd see you on the beach, running toward me, or in some crowd, looking right past me. Once, I saw a grown man who looked like me in a diner, and I swear it was you. I didn't go over because I didn't want to intrude, or maybe I didn't want to be rejected? Maybe I was still a coward.

Then, years later, I started becoming obsessed

with my boys. I couldn't get through a day without wanting to find you, to see you both.

When I did find you, I saw everything I'd missed: a man I helped bring into this world but didn't raise. A man shaped by the pain I'd caused... and all I felt was the need to "save your soul."

I was wrong. I needed you to save me.

I didn't walk away because I didn't want you; I walked away because I was terrified I'd ruin you.

By the time you needed me most, I was already too far gone.

You didn't just forgive me; you did so much more. You all accepted me, healed me, and allowed me to see what real life in the light can be. For that I will always be grateful.

If there's anything I've learned as a preacher, it's this: mercy doesn't erase what's been done, but it can rewrite what comes next.

Son,

If you are reading this, it means you made it. I wrote this because I was afraid I may never see you again. I wanted to explain and to tell you that I have always loved you; I was just lost. To finally be in your life and have this time as a part of your family has been

*the most surprising and rewarding gift. One that I
never saw coming. Thank you.*

I love you; I love you all.
Dad

**I read it under the light of an old kerosene
lantern** on the third day of our voyage. My
father had slipped it into the pack with our
journals and the ledger. It is the first time he
ever told me he loved me, and now I
understand.

I had good adopted parents, but nothing
compares to hearing that I was never disposable,
like I'd walked around my whole life believing.

So, thank you. I hope you read this. I hope
you know how much you mean to all of us and
how much you are missed. We love you as a
father, a grandpa "*Lolo,*" a teacher, a true man of
faith, and in the end — as the glue that kept us
together.

We couldn't have done it without you.

I love you too, Dad.

45.

Four years later, somewhere in the North Pacific...

I find myself so grateful in this final chapter, and it seemed unfair to leave our ending up to your imagination.

As I sit here writing these last words, my gaze stretches beyond the windowsill to the vast expanse of ocean. It's early morning, the mist has not yet lifted, and the sea is still wearing a hazy silver blanket. It reminds me of the first time I saw it, not just as water, but as something magnificent. Something sacred that gently claimed my brother.

We live above a little shop on the boardwalk. A shop we own.

To a tourist, it might seem modest or even plain. There are no flashing signs or polished fixtures, no mood music or sales chatter — but to us, it's nothing short of heaven.

It smells of fresh dough, warm fruit, clean

air, and something else — something you can't quite name but feel deep in your heart when you walk through the door.

We call it *Wallace's Mercantile*, though everyone in town calls it *"the shop."*

Inside, you'll find shelves lined with homemade jams and jellies, jars of candied nuts, infused honeys, and thick berry syrups. Leigh's sauces are legendary. People drive miles to get ahold of her green tomato relish or blackberry-pepper glaze.

Out front, wooden bins overflow with whatever's come up in the garden through the week: beets, tomatoes, squash, okra, or bundles of lavender wrapped in twine. We also sell fresh herbs. My wife's hands are never idle.

A small chalkboard reads, *"Today's Bread: Honey Oat & cinnamon raisin,"* and the scent of it baking lingers in the air well into the afternoon.

But the real heart of our shop is in the back, behind a blue curtain painted with gold moons and stitched stars. That's where Albert and Thomas work together most days, heads bent over their small workbench.

It's a strange, wonderful place filled with dried herbs hanging in clusters, tiny bottles of amber liquid, ceramic crocks and stone mortars, handwritten journals, and the faint sound of the radio. The boys, not so little now, have developed a sort of cottage alchemy.

Creams for aching joints. Wraps for swollen muscles. Drops for grief and salves for sleep, and somehow, it works.

Not just in the way good holistic medicine works, but in a way that leaves people smiling, wondering, and coming back.

Around the corner, two blocks from the shop, sits the town's community center. It's simple with its white walls, sloped roof, and paint that's always a little chipped from the salty air.

That's where Albert and I spend every afternoon each week, helping run support circles for cancer patients, addiction recovery, grief counseling, and others trying to hold on a little better or longer.

With time, we've grown fluent in several languages, and it's quite handy, especially in this area, where the sea brings people in from everywhere.

Don't get the wrong idea; we aren't on display here. We don't tell anyone what we really are. No stories of miracles, just quiet careful work… and occasionally, if someone is in need of relief, we walk them over to the shop to browse and share a cup of coffee or tea. You'd be surprised how much can be healed by a patient presence and a moment of understanding.

Himala is known throughout this little town for her smile, her kindness, and her way with animals. But what we know her for is the amazing ability she has at giving hugs to complete strangers. Especially children.

They trust her, and through her hands, the unsuspecting, scared, and weak receive light through a sweet embrace with an honesty that none of us can come close to.

She's famous for those long hugs, and sometimes, you'll see something change. Not immediately or explosively, but gently. She does it with a grace that makes the rest of us feel like students. She is pure in a way the world rarely gets to see twice.

We are safe here. We're part of a community, woven in with the fishermen and bakers, the weavers and musicians. Nobody asks too many questions. They wave hello when they pass, or they stop in for a purchase and usually give Thomas a hard time about his hair. We are loved, and we are happy. Not because we're different, but because we appear the same.

Except for our relationship with water, that's the only thing we must keep to ourselves.

We never all go in together — we can't — not in front of people; there's something too celestial about it. When we enter, the sea shifts around us. It remembers who we are, it knows us intimately, and it embraces us.

Every few weeks we drive out past the cliffs to a stretch of untouched shore where no one goes.

There, under the moon or sun or whatever sky we're given, we walk into the surf. We hold hands or dive together. We disappear beneath the surface like birds into a cloud, and when we rise again, we're stronger.

Whatever it is that lives inside of us glows brightest in those waters.

We draw from it, and we draw from each other. Love *is light*, and it really *does* conquer all.

So, if you ever find yourself wandering the Pacific coast and stumble across a crooked little shop with flowers in old teapots out front, come on in and say hello.

If Himala is there, she'll probably be sitting on a pillow with a rabbit or a kitten in her lap. If Albert and Thomas are bickering over how many cloves to put in a salve recipe, that's normal. If Leigh is sweeping the steps and singing an old hymn, you'll know you've come to the right place.

Please, just come on in; you're welcome.

You will leave with something warm in your chest and the faint scent of cinnamon, honeysuckle, or lavender on your sleeve.

And if it's a day that you need more, we are always eager to listen, have a meal, or even share a hug or a handshake. Your choice.

We'll be right here.

"You won't be the same, Scott. But that's the point. You weren't sent to stay the same; you were sent to become."

~Stan Wallace

Acknowledgments.

I loved writing this book. It has been written slowly over the last few years. I have a short list of people to thank. The first on that list is SHARKS BAY UMBI Diving Resort and Village. Sharm El Sheikh, Egypt. They are family, and I always seem to finish my work here. So, for Mr. Umbi, Hamid, Mohammed, Alaa, Zizo, and Rafaat, thank you for so much love and support. I need to thank my mom, who helped me write short stories as a young girl. To my computer formatting expert and friend who puts up with my fickle brain and helps me develop the pictures from my head into cover art, Riyaz Delilkhan, thanks for not giving up on me. I know I can be a lot to take sometimes. I need to thank my cousins who keep lifting me up and continue buying my books, never knowing what they are going to get! I keep a small circle, and the ones I've chosen to have in my life are the reason I keep writing. So, Robin Bolyn, Robin Martin, Ginnefer Cook-Gass, Joe Ferguson, Lee & Kimberly Mcgovern, Dr. Josephine Anis, and Omar Hayek, Thank you.

In this fiercely personal memoir, Jamie Lee Carrie invites you into a world marked by beauty and brutality, laughter and loss, silence and survival. From the suburbs of Texas to the rooftops of Egypt, she weaves a story not just of pain—but of persistence. Not just of what was taken—but what still bloomed. Told with unflinching honesty and flashes of unexpected grace, *Blooming After the Blaze* is the true account of a woman who refused to stay broken. It's not a story about running from the past—it's about what you find when you finally stop and face it. It's faith, hard work, and resilience in real time, and it might just make you believe in yourself.
Some seeds only bloom after fire.

BLOOMING AFTER THE BLAZE:
Five Years on the Run

For decades, the *urban legend* made its way through Egypt, surrounding countries, and beyond. It had even captured the attention of the Nazi regime in the 1930s, and they tirelessly searched.

It was the tale of a young Egyptian prince born in the 1700's named Alaa. An arranged marriage, an eventual love that was all consuming— of a difficult pregnancy, an impossible birth, and the loss of both mother and child. Unimaginable pain and grief, and an elaborate tomb built into the side of a cliff in an undisclosed location in Cairo. The death of a king and an inheritance of **5 stones** that would allow five possibilities for redemption.

This story takes place in London, Scotland, and Egypt in 2019.

FIVE STONES: Alaa's Quest

When high-powered attorney Heath Parker finds himself in debt to the Mafia, he plans his wife's kidnapping, hoping her tragic death will clear his slate, while simultaneously making him a very wealthy man.

Leo was not a criminal, but he'd agreed to the task. The fact was, the people Allison Parker's husband owed were the exact same people that Leo's father did. The assignment was the only way to keep his family safe; he had no choice. If he failed, it would mean death for all of them, including his mother and little sister. He wasn't doing it for family honor; he was doing it for their survival. Disposing of a middle-aged, spoiled, and miserable woman would save four lives. And the way he looked at it, he was probably doing her a favor.

But what is supposed to be a quick and cold-hearted transaction changes when a snowstorm entraps them together, captor and hostage, secluded for months from the outside world.

Forced into close quarters, their isolation breeds unexpected and mutual desire and at some point, she becomes worth the risk--worth saving.

As Leo watches snow fall relentlessly outside the cabin window, he knows *he can't kill her*. But he doesn't know how to save her either.

He doesn't know how to save *any of them*.

LICKING THE KNIFE

AMAZON AUTHORS QR CODE